INFINITY RING

"We're members of a group called the Hystorians," the man said. "You wouldn't have heard of us, but our organization goes back many, many centuries. It was founded by the great philosopher Aristotle in 336 BCE. We've lasted in a continuous line ever since, united in a common goal to set right the world's course...before everything ends in the fiery Cataclysm that Aristotle himself predicted. Today you've given us the biggest breakthrough since he spoke of that vision. Time travel."

He paused and gave a long look to Sera, then Dak. **"History is broken, and we need your help to fix it."**

$2\underline{\overline{3}}$

②

OPERATION TRINITY

CAHILL THE 39 CLUES FILES

CLIFFORD RILEY

SCHOLASTIC INC.
NEW YORK TORONTO LONDON AUCKLAND
SYDNEY MEXICO CITY NEW DELHI HONG KONG

The author would like to acknowledge
Mallory Kass for her words,
and Rachel Griffiths for her wisdom.
—C.R.

Library of Congress Control Number: 2012931145

ISBN 978-0-545-43143-9
10 9 8 7 6 5 4 3 2 1   12 13 14 15 16

Book design by Charice Silverman
First edition, May 2012
Printed in the U.S.A.   23

Scholastic US: 557 Broadway • New York, NY 10012
Scholastic Canada: 604 King Street West • Toronto, ON M5V 1E1
Scholastic New Zealand Limited: Private Bag 94407 • Greenmount, Manukau 2141
Scholastic UK Ltd.: Euston House • 24 Eversholt Street • London NW1 1DB

McIntyre, MacArthur, Mulligan & Smood

ATTORNEYS AT LAW

To whom it may concern,

The information in this book comes from the Cahill vault, which means that *none* of it was meant for your eyes. Over the past 500 years, a number of exceedingly dangerous items have been placed in the vault for safekeeping—assassination orders, confession-filled diaries, treasure maps, and many other items that I know better than to list here. Documents that have sparked wars, incited revolutions, and led to the downfall of governments, kings, and empires.

It was *not* my idea to make this material public. I was given specific instructions by my former employer, William McIntyre, to protect the information in the vault. However, after recent, tragic events, it looks like I'm taking orders from someone new—someone who believes that the Cahill Files are essential to the security of the Cahill family . . . and the world at large.

And so, the vault has been opened. Do with these stories what you will. But when you find yourself weighed down by the secrets and scandals that shaped history, just remember one thing: I told you so.

Clifford Riley

PART 1

Ghent, 1566

Matheus Jacobs scraped his spoon along the side of the wooden bowl, filling it with flakes of dried stew. Once he finished his supper, his visit home would be over and he'd have to start his long ride back to the cathedral.

He turned to the window. The sun was already beginning to set, flooding the wheat field with soft orange light. His father and his oldest brother, Adriaan, were out there somewhere, trying to coax the plants from the barren ground.

Since Adriaan would inherit the family land, the younger boys had to learn a trade. Lukas was already apprenticed to the local blacksmith, and Matheus had assumed that he'd also be sent to work when he turned thirteen next year. But instead of finding him a job with the village baker or carpenter, his mother had arranged for him to serve as an altar boy at Saint Bavo Cathedral in Ghent—a morning's ride on a proper horse, a half day on their poky mule, Mungo.

"Are you almost ready, *beertje*?" his mother, Anna, called from the back of the room, where she was tucking baby Greetje into her cradle.

Matheus scrunched his face, although he secretly liked it when his mother called him "little bear," a reference to the dark, curly hair that distinguished him from his blond brothers.

"You need to hurry if you want to get to the city before dark," Anna said. Matheus looked down to keep his mother from seeing the blush spreading across his cheeks. His hair wasn't all that set him apart. He was the only one of his brothers who was afraid of the dark—who was afraid of anything, really.

That was probably why he'd been sent to the cathedral instead of being apprenticed. He was an embarrassment. Matheus's father, Joost, had no patience for his spindly, clumsy son, who could barely haul a full bucket of water without drenching his tunic. He'd seen the shame in his father's face when Matheus limped home after losing a fight.

Before Matheus could reply, there was a knock at the front entrance. That was odd. The family and their neighbors always came through the kitchen. "Go see who it is, *beertje*," Anna called. Matheus lifted the latch and pulled open the heavy door, revealing a tall, slender man in a strange outfit. Instead of a tunic and trousers, he wore a brocade jacket over knee breeches and white silk stockings. At first, Matheus wondered how the man had managed to stay so clean, but then he heard the stomp of a hoof. An elegant carriage pulled by four matching dappled grays had stopped in the middle of the road.

"Is this the Jacobs home?" the man asked. He had a strange accent, and he grimaced slightly as he spoke, as if the foreign words left a sour taste in his mouth.

Matheus nodded.

The man removed a letter from the pouch hanging at his hip. "Are you quite sure?" He raised an eyebrow. "It's treason to tamper with a message from the king."

The king? Then perhaps the messenger *was* looking for another Jacobs family. Surely King Philip wouldn't have business with his parents.

"Who is it?" Anna's voice called from behind him. Matheus stepped aside to let his mother pass. "Can I help you?" she asked, wiping her hands on her apron.

"I have a letter for Mevrouw Jacobs," the messenger said with a note of irritation in his voice.

"I am Mevrouw Jacobs."

"Mevrouw *Anna* Jacobs?" he asked, giving her an appraising look. "I have come a long way, and I do not intend to leave His Majesty's correspondence with some peasant."

Matheus saw his mother stiffen next to him. She raised her chin. "*¿Está de España?*" she said in a language he'd never heard before.

The messenger's cheeks flushed slightly. "I do not speak Spanish, madam."

"You're not from the king's court in Madrid."

"I took over for His Majesty's courier in France."

"Donc, je suis Anna Jacobs. Donnez-moi le lettre, s'il vous plaît."

Both the messenger and Matheus stared at her wide-eyed. The only people he'd heard speak anything but Dutch were the priests, who chanted in Latin, and the traders at the market. Yet here was his mother conversing in foreign tongues like a queen.

The messenger handed Anna the letter, bowed his head, and then strode back to his carriage. Matheus turned to his mother slowly, half expecting to find that she'd turned into someone else completely. But there she was. The same large brown eyes and rosy cheeks. "What's going on?" he asked.

"Not here," she whispered, glancing down the road before guiding Matheus inside and closing the door. She held up the letter and examined the elaborate wax seal. Instead of the royal coat of arms he'd seen emblazoned on proclamations and flags, there was a large C. His mother had taught him to read and write, but he couldn't think what the initial could stand for.

Anna carefully broke the seal and unfolded the letter, pressing her lips together as her eyes traveled across the paper. Her face was tight, as if the muscles were straining to keep some private thought from spilling onto her face.

"Mother, why is the king sending *you* letters?" Matheus asked. "And how do you speak all those languages?" A prickle of dread formed in his stomach. "Are we in trouble?" he asked as terrifying images began to spill out from the dark places in his memory. Over the past year, news of unrest in other parts of the land had reached their village. Protestant dissenters were speaking out against the Catholic Church and Spanish rule. There were rumors that the king's army had begun arresting people during rallies, or taking them away in the middle of the night.

Yet his family was Catholic, and he'd never heard either of his parents speak ill of the Crown.

Anna closed her eyes for a moment and then took a breath. "There's something I have to tell you."

The back door slammed, and Matheus jumped. His father, Joost, stormed into the room, leaving a trail of dirty boot prints in his wake. "What's going on?" he boomed. "I saw a carriage leaving."

"It was a message from the king." Anna held up the letter. "He thinks *it's* in danger."

"*What's* in danger?" Matheus asked. His heart sped up, sending a mixture of fear and frustration coursing through his body.

"Watch your tone," his father snapped.

"It's fine, Joost," Anna said, clasping his arm. "It's time to tell him." She took a step forward toward her son. "There's a special reason we sent you to be an altar boy, Matheus." She shot a quick glance toward the window. "It's about the altarpiece."

Matheus had been waiting for his mother to say

something that would shine a light on the fog that had settled over him since the messenger arrived, but her words only served to thicken the haze of confusion. Saint Bavo Cathedral was home to a magnificent altarpiece—a series of twenty-four paintings by the renowned Jan van Eyck. The work was heralded as a masterpiece—one of the world's great treasures. Artists traveled great distances to study Van Eyck's technique. What could the altarpiece possibly have to do with Matheus's mother?

"My grandmother came from England specifically to protect the altarpiece. And ever since then, one of her descendants has watched over it."

"Protect it from whom?" Matheus asked.

"There's a dangerous group called the Vespers that's been trying to steal the altarpiece for decades. And it's up to our family—the Cahills—to keep it safe."

It was as if she were still speaking one of those foreign languages for all the sense her words made to Matheus. "Why us? Wouldn't the Church protect it?"

Anna shook her head. "They know nothing about the threat. The Vespers are masters at operating from the shadows." She held up the letter. "The king's Cahill advisers believe that the Vespers are behind the current rebellion, and are going to use it to seize the paintings. That's why we need someone in the cathedral at all times." She gave him a small smile and ruffled his hair. "Like an altar boy."

Matheus took a step back. "But what am I supposed to do to protect it?" He'd never won so much as a wrestling match. How was he supposed to fend off a mysterious enemy?

Joost sighed and placed his hand on Anna's shoulder, turning her away slightly. "I told you he was the wrong choice," he murmured. "Send Lukas. He's still young enough to be an altar boy."

His words burned Matheus's ears, and then spread to his chest like a growing flame. He knew his father was disappointed with him, but hearing proof was worse than he could have imagined, like waking up after a terrifying dream only to find the creature from your nightmare standing next to your bed.

"He's the one," his mother said firmly, returning to face Matheus. "The Vespers aren't an invading army you can crush with superior strength. That's what makes them so dangerous."

"Lukas stands a better chance."

"It's my family's responsibility, Joost. And we've chosen Matheus."

Joost stared at her for a moment. "I hope you know what you're doing," he said, placing his cap on his head. "I must be off." He nodded at Matheus. "Do your best, boy. We're all counting on you."

Anna watched him leave, and then walked over to fetch Matheus's cloak from the peg by the back door. "Don't listen to him," she said as she draped the rough wool over his shoulders. "I know you'll make me proud, Matheus." She gave him a final kiss, opened the door, and ushered him out into the fading light.

"Come *on*!" Matheus half shouted, half groaned as he thumped his legs against Mungo's sides. But the mule ignored his rider's exasperated kicks and continued munching on the patch of clover he'd spotted off the road. It was the fourth snack break the beast had initiated in less than a mile. It wouldn't even matter *how* Matheus was supposed to guard the altarpiece, if he never even made it back to Ghent.

The wind had picked up, and the skin on his neck and face began to sting. He reached down and stroked the coarse hair on the mule's neck. "Please? If you get me back before dark, I'll give you a carrot." Mungo twitched his long ears, but kept chewing. "And a big, juicy apple." The mule raised his head and snorted, spraying wet flecks of clover onto the toe of Matheus's left boot.

Matheus sat perfectly still as the animal's muscles twitched experimentally. It was crucial that Mungo feel it was his decision to continue. With a resigned whinny, the mule lumbered back onto the path.

Matheus sighed as he loosened the reins. Mungo was going to choose his own pace, anyway. As they turned down the road through the village, the mule broke into a surprisingly animated trot. His belly jiggled with each step, making it difficult for Matheus to keep his balance.

They rounded the bend, and Matheus's stomach

flipped. A group of boys about his age was standing in a circle, hooting and hollering as they watched a wrestling match. Matheus slouched deeper in the saddle and tugged the hood of his cloak around his face. But it was no use. They'd seen him.

Normally, the Protestant and Catholic children in the village got along, or at least left each other alone. But over the past few months, fights had been breaking out. Most of his neighbors knew Matheus was an altar boy, which made him a target.

"Look, it's the choirboy!" a gangly lad shouted to his friends.

Matheus's neighbor, Pieter, took a step forward. "Where's your harp, angel?"

Matheus gave Mungo a firm squeeze with his calves, but the mule chose that moment to go investigate some apples rotting in the gutter. Matheus yanked on the reins with all his might, yet he couldn't stop the mule from rushing headlong toward the fruit. He skidded to a stop on the slippery road, and Matheus tumbled off into a puddle of mud and decaying apples.

The boys roared with laughter. "Still think you're something special, altar boy?" the tall boy called.

Matheus ignored them as he tried to remount, but his boots were covered with mud and his foot kept sliding out of the stirrup. After a few failed attempts, he grabbed the grimy reins and hauled Mungo away from the apples. He climbed onto a wooden crate and then swung his leg over the saddle. Matheus dug his heels into the mule's bloated sides and urged him to walk forward.

The boys' laughter echoed through the village square, but Matheus could barely hear them. All he could focus on was the man standing in front of the tavern, staring at him with a look of bitter disappointment.

Matheus tucked his chin into his tunic and stared at the ground as he rode by. He'd pretend he hadn't seen his father. And his father could pretend he only had two sons.

Matheus couldn't sleep. It was hard to trade the sleepy warmth of his snug house for the chill of the drafty dormitory. The wind always kept him awake like a restless bedfellow, tossing and turning in the night.

But the strange noises were the least of Matheus's worries. His mother's words echoed through his brain, drowning all other sounds. Matheus was in charge of protecting the altarpiece. But what did that mean? Was he supposed to pace back and forth in front of it all night, waving a club in the air? Matheus didn't think the sexton would be too pleased with that option. And what would he do if someone did try to steal it? He couldn't bear to recall the look he'd seen on his father's face, and tried to shove the memory into the darkest corner of his mind. But he could still feel its sharp edge piercing through his thoughts.

The loud, even breathing of his fellow altar boys

filled him with envy. They didn't have mothers who gave them bizarre, impossible tasks. They didn't have fathers who expected them to fail.

Matheus looked up at the narrow window across from his cot. A full moon wobbled in the corner, distorted by the thick glass. It was past midnight, which meant that the sanctuary would be empty.

It was time to check on the altarpiece.

Matheus rose and padded quietly toward the door, wincing as the cold from the floor seeped into his bare feet and crept up his legs. The long hallway was dark, but the moon provided just enough light for Matheus to find his way down to the first floor. He scurried across the courtyard and snuck in through the chapter house, where the bishop met with important visitors, and then darted past the cloisters into the front hall.

Matheus paused as he reached the entrance to the sanctuary. It was strange being there alone — normally, the cathedral was full of worshippers, priests, nuns, and altar boys. He took a step forward into the vast nave, the heart of the church. It looked even larger in the dark. The long center aisle seemed to stretch out interminably, and the pulpit at the end was hardly visible in the dim light.

Yet although Matheus generally hated the dark, there was something reassuring about the cathedral at night. During the day, the sun shone through the stained glass windows, filling the life-sized saints with a holy glow that made Matheus bow his head in reverence. But at night, the moonlight filtering through the panes made the figures look almost human.

As he walked down the aisle, passing the empty pews and dark alcoves that housed smaller altars and stone crypts, even the shadows were more comforting than menacing. The same shapes unfurled across the black-and-white floor every night like nocturnal flowers that lived for centuries. Time seemed to stand still in the cathedral. There was no changing of seasons. No cycles of birth and death. The air was always heavy with the smell of incense, the echo of music, and the memory of muttered prayers.

When he finally reached the pulpit, Matheus knelt and crossed himself before rising and turning to face the altarpiece. Even in the dim light, it took his breath away. The hinged panels were open, so the inner panels were visible — twelve paintings of different sizes that had been connected to form a screen. All together, the entire piece was larger than the front of his house.

Matheus's eyes first traveled to the middle panel, where the figure of God was looking down from his golden throne. A shiver ran down his spine and he tilted his head to look at the large scene on the bottom panel, the most celebrated painting in the altarpiece — "The Adoration of the Mystic Lamb." Van Eyck had portrayed the moment before the sacrifice. The lamb stood proudly on a pedestal in a green field, surrounded by angels. Groups of worshippers watched from a respectful distance. A sun shone down on the assembled crowd, and standing in the drafty, dark cathedral, Matheus could imagine the warmth on his skin.

Van Eyck had spent six years on the twenty-four individual paintings, and the detail was spectacular. Each of the hundreds of figures had a unique face and a distinct expression. The saints' robes fell in lustrous folds onto the grass. Strange, exotic foliage bloomed in the background. Matheus could only imagine how far someone would have to travel in order to see plants like that. Although there was no proof that Van Eyck had left the Netherlands, there were rumors that his patron, the Duke of Burgundy, had sent the artist to faraway lands on court business. Could those journeys have anything to do with the Vespers?

Matheus squinted to examine something he had only found the other day. One of the figures in the bottom left panel had strange symbols embroidered onto his cap. They looked like letters, but they weren't in a language Matheus had ever seen.

A loud *thump* shook the silence of the sanctuary. Matheus felt his heart flutter as he spun around. Could an attack be happening already? He spread his arms to the side, like a goose shielding a flock of goslings. Except that his spindly limbs would hardly stop a fly from landing on the altarpiece.

There was another *thump*, followed by the sound of metal hitting stone.

There was someone in the sanctuary.

"Who's there?" Matheus croaked, cringing at how faint and wobbly his voice sounded in the vast cathedral. There wasn't even an echo. He cleared his throat and tried again. "Reveal yourself!"

He looked around desperately for a weapon, but there was nothing. In a moment of panic, he darted behind one of the columns and hid there, shaking.

A flicker of light fluttered through the darkness. Matheus peeked out from behind the column and saw a figure holding a candle.

Do something! Matheus's brain screamed at him, but his feet remained firmly planted on the ground.

"Hello?" a deep voice rang out. Instead of being absorbed by the mass of silence, it pushed off the walls like a great bird gliding from perch to perch.

Matheus stepped into the quivering pool of light cast by the candle, and exhaled when he saw that the figure was wearing the vestments of a priest. Although it was difficult to tell in the dark, Matheus was fairly sure he'd never seen the man before. "Good evening, Father," he said respectfully.

"Hello," the priest replied. It was unclear whether he was angry or just surprised to find an altar boy lurking in the sanctuary so late. "And who might you be?"

"My name is Matheus Jacobs."

"Ah. I'm Father Gerard. I was just transferred from Bruges, you see. I suppose I'm still getting used to my new surroundings. It can be difficult falling asleep in a new home." He waved his arm through the shadowy air. "Even one as magnificent as this."

"I couldn't sleep, either," Matheus said, relieved that wandering through the chilly cathedral in the middle of the night seemed to be an acceptable cure for sleeplessness. "I had a dream that the altarpiece was in danger, so I came to check on it."

The priest stared at him for a moment before chuckling. "I see. How very conscientious." He took a step forward. "Although there is no cause for concern."

"Of course, Father."

"And it's probably better for you to stay in the dormitory, Matheus. We can't have small boys traipsing around at night, even well-intentioned ones."

Matheus felt his cheeks flush. "Yes, Father."

The priest smiled. "Good night, my son."

Matheus scurried back up the aisle. When he reached the top, he paused and glanced over his shoulder. The priest remained facing the altarpiece. In the darkness, the outline of his robes blended with the shadows, making him look more like a statue than a man, as if he, too, were as much a part of the cathedral as the windows and the stone.

Matheus stepped into the sunlight and squinted, adjusting the heavy basket in his arms in an attempt to find a better grip. After breakfast that morning, Father Gerard had pulled Matheus aside with instructions for an errand. A family in a nearby village had just lost a child, and Father Gerard was sending them a basket of food.

Although Matheus had explained that only the older altar boys were allowed to go that far from the cathedral, the priest had insisted. He figured it would be good for Matheus—the journey would tire him out enough that he wouldn't have any more trouble sleeping. He must have noticed the look of uncertainty on Matheus's face, because he'd smiled and said, "You can take my horse, Brutus. He could use the exercise."

As Matheus trudged down the narrow alley that led from the kitchen to the stables, he felt a mix of excitement and apprehension. He was happy to abandon his cleaning and polishing duties for the day, but it seemed wrong to leave the altarpiece unattended after yesterday's strange events. Yet what harm could possibly befall it in the middle of the day?

Mungo was in the livestock pen, lying on the ground with his hairy legs in the air as he wriggled in the mud, trying to scratch a hard-to-reach spot on his back. When he saw Matheus, he rolled onto his side and clambered to his feet. He pricked his ears and stared at Matheus, a muddy, four-legged soldier at attention. "Sorry, Mungo," he called. "Not today."

The mule trotted over and stuck his neck through the fence to nuzzle Matheus's sleeve. He gave Mungo a quick scratch on the nose and then pushed him away. "I'm not taking you. You're too slow." His destination was on the outskirts of the city, near his family's village, and he wasn't in the mood to spend another four hours begging the lazy animal to move.

He darted into the stable, where the high-ranking clergymen's horses were kept, tacked up Brutus, a fine-boned bay, and led him into the yard. It was a little difficult to mount the tall horse holding a basket of food with one arm, especially once Brutus began whinnying and prancing in place. But Matheus eventually managed to hoist himself into the saddle.

Mungo snorted from his pen and stamped his hoof. "Everything's fine," Matheus said to the mule as he gathered up Brutus's reins. "I'll be back soon." He gave Brutus a nudge with his heels, and the horse took off at a canter, scattering a flock of chickens into the air.

Matheus grinned as they flew down the narrow alley, splashing through the mud and swerving to avoid the maids emptying washbasins out of back windows. As they turned sharply out of the yard and onto the main road, Brutus lengthened into a gallop. It was exhilarating to feel the wind streaming over his face and to listen to the rapid thud of Brutus's hooves as they swallowed the ground. If only his father could see him, thundering along the canal with his white altar boy robes streaming in the wind. Surely he looked worthy of protecting the altarpiece now.

By the time he reached his destination and delivered the basket, it was late afternoon, his favorite time of day. The landscape grew more confident in its beauty; the green of the hills stopped straining to upstage the blue sky, and the colors became softer, more harmonious.

Matheus shortened his reins and asked Brutus for a trot. If he hurried, he'd have time to visit the market outside of his village. Although Matheus had no money of his own to spend, it was fun to examine the wide array of goods — the mounds of red apples, the heaps of fresh fish, and silk all the way from the East.

Yet as he rounded the bend that led to the market, it wasn't the sound of bargaining or the smell of roasting meat that caught Matheus's attention.

A man was standing on a pile of wooden crates, surrounded by a crowd. He was giving some sort of speech, although it was difficult to make out the words. After nearly everything he said, the audience responded with cheers or shouts of their own.

"Will we allow the king to persecute our brothers?"

A number of people shook their heads while murmurs of disapproval rippled through the assembly.

"Are we going to sit idly by while the Church festers with the corruption of human greed?"

"No!" a few people replied.

Matheus brought Brutus to an abrupt halt, though his heart continued to beat rapidly. He knew he should turn around and take another route back to Ghent. In his altar boy robes, he was the last person the crowd would be happy to see. Yet there was something magnetic about the speaker. It was scary, but also a little exciting to see regular people — farmers, laborers, and merchants — talk about religion with such passion.

"Just last week, our brave brothers and sisters in Antwerp took it upon themselves to stand up for righteousness. They stormed the cathedral!" The audience cheered. "They burned the heretical art."

Matheus's stomach twisted as a wave of applause and cheers surged through the square. The mood of the gathering was shifting quickly.

A man standing in front of Matheus cleared his throat. He was tall, and wore a black hat and a black traveling cloak. "The cathedral in Ghent has even more treasures!" he shouted, his voice soaring over the crowd. "If we want to prove our might, we should destroy them as well."

A look of concern flashed across the speaker's face. "Well, perhaps it would be best to wait —"

"We cannot afford to wait. We've been suffering at their hands for too long." The man in the cloak raised his chin. He was so tall that he didn't need to stand on anything to be seen by most of the audience. "Now is the time to stand together, to show them our power."

"Hear, hear!" a man called from the other side of the square, sparking a flurry of nods and murmurs.

"We will show them what we think of their idols," the man in the cloak spat. "We'll burn the symbols of their greed. All the paintings. Their beloved altarpiece."

Matheus gasped, but the sound was lost in the frenzy of cheers.

"Friends, please," the original speaker said. "I urge you to—"

The man in the cloak cut him off. "And we will destroy anyone who stands in our way!"

"We'll start here!" a woman Matheus vaguely recognized shouted. "The Catholics in our village need to be taught a lesson!"

The audience began to stream onto the road, but the cloaked man remained in place, surveying the scene with a serene smile. As the square emptied, he walked toward the other side and disappeared into the shadows. But Matheus didn't have time to worry about where he might be going.

Something terrible was about to happen. The mob was already moving toward Ghent—on a path that would take them straight through his village.

Matheus tugged on the reins and sent Brutus forward.

He wasn't sure which was in graver danger: the altarpiece—

Or his family.

Matheus and Brutus tore through the woods, scrambling down slippery hills and through thick brush. But as they rounded the bend that led to the village, Brutus skidded to an abrupt stop. Matheus winced as he landed on the horse's neck before righting himself with a groan. "Come *on*," he said, gritting his teeth as he tried to kick Brutus forward.

But the horse just raised his elegant brown head and snorted, flicking his ears nervously.

That's when Matheus smelled the smoke.

He shortened the reins and gave Brutus a firm squeeze, sending the horse into a stiff-legged walk. They turned the corner and Matheus inhaled sharply.

A different mass of people had already gathered in front of a small house. The roof was on fire. But instead of fetching water or trying to stamp it out, the crowd was shouting.

"Burn the infidels!" someone yelled, prompting a chorus of cheers.

The attacks had begun.

With a surge of dread, Matheus nudged Brutus into a canter, steering him off the road to pass the crowd of people. He continued around a bend, and when he was sure the path was clear, urged the horse into a gallop.

It'll be all right, he told himself, as they tore along the tree-lined path that led to his house. *It'll be all right*. He repeated these words in time to the rhythm of Brutus's pounding hooves. *It'll be all right*. He'd be able to warn his family before the mob arrived. They were on foot. He was on horseback.

He thought about the woman he'd seen in front of the burning house. The look of horror and heartbreak on her face as she saw her home destroyed.

That's not going to happen to us.

They galloped up the hill that led to the village. The sun was low on the horizon, and he could see the glow of lanterns floating in the twilit haze.

Yet as Brutus tore up the hill, sending chunks of dirt flying in all directions, the lights grew brighter. They weren't lanterns.

They were torches.

The mob must have cut through the wheat fields.

He was too late.

As Matheus steered Brutus toward his house, everything fell oddly silent. He couldn't hear the crackle of the torches, or any shouts that might have been ringing out in the distance. All he could hear was the thud of Brutus's hooves and the beat of his own heart.

There were already people outside. They were blocking the windows, so Matheus couldn't tell whether anyone was still in the house.

The door opened, and Matheus's father stepped outside. "What do you want?" Joost barked. Yet despite his harsh tone, there was fear in his eyes.

"We want you to stop defiling our city with your sinful ways," a man said, prompting a round of cheers.

While the crowd shouted, a group of figures crept along the side of the house, toward the back entrance.

Matheus was about to follow them when a loud *crack* commanded his attention.

Joost ducked as a large rock came hurtling toward him, bouncing off the doorframe and landing on the ground with a heavy thud.

There was a flurry of movement as the mob scoured the path for more stones.

Right in front of Matheus, a large man with huge muscles straining against his tunic raised his arms and hoisted a melon-sized rock above his head.

"No!" Matheus shouted, jabbing Brutus with his heels. But the horse balked, unwilling to go anywhere near the loud mob with their flickering torches. He snorted and spun around on his back hooves.

Without thinking, Matheus launched out of the saddle and wrapped his arm around the man's beefy neck. He released the stone as he thrashed around, trying to shake the boy off. Matheus kneed him in the stomach, and then dropped to the ground as the man hunched forward, clasping his belly.

He dashed through the crowd, pulling his father through the door before the mob had a chance to react.

"Matheus?" Joost said, as if he couldn't quite believe that the boy standing in front of him was his son.

"Where's Mother?" Matheus asked, frantically scanning the main room.

"Oh, *beertje*," she said, rushing from the bedroom carrying Greet. "What are you doing here?"

Matheus ran to her, throwing his arm around her waist. "Are the windows locked? They might try to come in through the back."

"Yes," Anna said, placing Greet in her cradle. "We had a feeling this might happen. That's why it was so important for you to guard the altarpiece." Matheus's chest tightened as he heard the panic and frustration in her voice.

"The priest sent me on an errand. I saw the mob form." He took a breath, but all the words he was desperate to say seemed to be stuck in his throat.

"Which priest?"

"A new one . . . Father Gerard." As soon as the name left his lips, a wave of cold passed over him. How could he have been so foolish? Father Gerard hadn't just been taking a walk last night. He hadn't sent Matheus away to be nice. He'd been trying to keep him away from the altarpiece.

He was a Vesper.

"I'm so sorry," Matheus said hoarsely. "I didn't know . . . I never should have . . ."

"It's fine," Anna said, placing her arm around him. "As soon as it's safe, you'll head back. It's not too late."

"No," Matheus cried. The energy that had fueled his high-speed journey was gone. Now all he felt was weak and empty. "I'm not leaving."

Joost walked over and placed his hand on Matheus's shoulder. "You've shown extraordinary bravery tonight. I need you to stay strong and listen to your mother."

A few hours ago, hearing his father speak those words would've filled Matheus with joy, but now all he could think about was the torchlight shining through the windows. The shouts and stamps that seemed to be rocking the very foundation of the house.

The three of them leaped up as a loud *smash* filled the room. Matheus felt his stomach plummet into his toes as a figure appeared in the doorway to the bedroom, shaking shards of glass from his sleeves.

It was the man in the black cloak.

"Excuse the intrusion," he said, stepping into the main room. He had a slight foreign accent that Matheus hadn't noticed earlier. "I would've used the front door, but I didn't want to interrupt the festivities."

Anna inhaled sharply. "You're one of them, aren't you? A Vesper." Her tone was equal parts fear and incredulity, as if she were addressing a creature that was only supposed to exist in legends.

Joost stepped forward. "What are you doing in our home?"

"I was planning on paying a little visit to Saint Bavo this evening. I heard the altarpiece is even more striking by candlelight. And then it came to my attention that you might be able to *illuminate* the paintings for me even further." He smiled. "You see, I am no expert on art, and I would very much appreciate any assistance you could provide."

"We don't know anything," Anna said firmly.

The man gave an exaggerated sigh. "I was afraid you were going to say that." He reached into his cloak and produced a long dagger. Matheus winced, as if the image itself were enough to slice his eyes.

The man whistled, and two more people stepped in from the bedroom. A man and a woman, both dressed all in black. The woman was wearing breeches instead of a skirt, but her strange ensemble was overshadowed by the cruel smile that played across her long, thin face.

"Tell me how the map works, and we'll leave peacefully. I'll even get the crowd to disperse." The man's gaze slid toward Greet's cradle. "Otherwise, you'll just make things difficult for yourselves."

"I don't know," Anna said, unable to hide the desperation in her voice.

The man looked over his shoulder and cocked his head toward the cradle. His two accomplices strode toward Matheus and Joost, and before either of them had time to react, forced their hands behind their backs.

"Get off me!" Matheus shouted, twisting painfully as he attempted to kick the woman's shin with his heel. But she held tight.

The man took a few steps forward and started to reach into Greet's cradle.

"*No!*" Anna screamed in a voice that was not her own. It was hardly human, a noise that contained all the agony in the world. She lunged for the man, jabbing her elbow into his throat. He gagged as he grabbed her wrist, and plunged the blade into her chest.

She gasped but didn't scream, and for a moment,

Matheus was convinced he'd seen it wrong. It was a trick of light. The dagger hadn't touched her. Everything was going to be fine.

But then Anna fell backward onto the floor, landing with a thud that Matheus felt in his chest.

His father sank to his knees and stared mutely, as if not wanting to desecrate his wife's last cry with sounds of his own.

"Search the house," the man said. The woman in the black breeches released Matheus's arms.

He ran toward Anna, skidding on his knees as he bent down.

"Mother." He ran his hand along her cheek, which was just as warm and rosy as it had always been. She must have just fainted. She was going to be fine.

His eyes traveled down her still body until they reached the handle of the dagger sticking out of her chest, surrounded by an expanding circle of crimson. He stared at it uncomprehendingly, like he did when he came across a word he didn't understand in the Bible. His brain couldn't process the image. It didn't make sense. It couldn't be real.

"Mother," he said, gently shaking her shoulder. "It's fine. They're leaving." He glanced around the room. They must have gone into the bedroom. "We'll get you help now."

"Go," his father croaked, pushing himself onto his knees. "Go now. They're heading for the altarpiece."

Matheus grabbed Anna's hand. "Get up, Mother. We need to leave."

"Matheus," his father said, his voice cracking. "You have to go!"

He released his mother's hand and watched it fall limply to the floor. He sat back on his heels as he felt a tight numbness spread through his chest, as if his rib cage was trying to squeeze his heart to death.

She was gone.

"Matheus!" his father cried. "Please." A sob broke through him. "It's what she would have wanted."

He rose shakily to his feet and looked at his father. Joost nodded.

Matheus turned to his mother one last time, although it was difficult to see her from behind the warm tears that had begun welling up in his eyes.

He wiped his face on the sleeve and headed toward the door.

Matheus slipped out the side window. The mob was still in front of the house, but they had spread out along the road. They seemed to be awaiting instructions from the man in the black cloak.

He looked around. Brutus was nowhere to be seen.

He was entirely alone.

Suddenly, Matheus's boots felt so heavy he didn't think he could take another step.

His mother was dead. The altarpiece was in jeopardy. And he was ten miles away, with no way of getting back to Ghent.

The world began to spin, and Matheus had to grab on to a fence for balance. He wanted to sit down. He wanted to go to sleep and wake up when this was all over — or never wake up at all.

He was about to close his eyes when a shape emerged from the darkness. A four-legged shape . . . with very large ears.

It was Mungo.

From the shards of wood embedded in his curly hair, it looked like he had broken through the fence of his pen at the cathedral. And from the mud that covered his stocky legs, it looked like he'd been in a hurry to get here. Matheus didn't know if the mule had come to find him, or if he'd been looking for food, but he didn't care. He flung his arms around Mungo's neck as his tears spilled into his rough mane.

"Grab that boy!" a voice shouted. Matheus spun around. It was the woman in the breeches.

Holding on to the mane for balance, Matheus climbed onto the fence and leaped onto Mungo's bare back. Before he even had time to squeeze the mule's sides, Mungo took off.

"Stop him!" the woman bellowed.

There was a flurry of stomps as a number of people began running after Matheus. He glanced over his shoulder and saw a few of the men jump onto horses of their own and begin tearing down the road after them.

Matheus crouched down over Mungo's neck, urging him forward. The mule stretched out into his best approximation of a gallop. Matheus slipped from side to side with every beat, latching on with his legs for dear life.

Mungo's top speed was no match for the horses pursuing them. Matheus could hear the hoofbeats growing closer, their rapid thud outpaced only by the frantic beat of his heart.

It was difficult to steer without a bridle, but guiding Mungo with his heels, Matheus was able to urge the mule off the main road and onto a trail that led through the woods. The canopy of leaves was so dense it blocked out the last of the fading light, making it seem like they were galloping into an abyss.

Matheus heard the horses behind them whinny in protest, but Mungo was undaunted, and charged on.

A flurry of shouts and cracking whips broke through the sounds of pounding hooves and panting horses.

They were getting closer.

Up ahead was a stone wall that ran along the canal. If he could figure out a way to get around it — and convince Mungo to go in the water — they'd be able to use it as a shortcut to Ghent.

The trees thinned out as they got closer to the edge. In the faint light, Matheus could see the wall grow larger. He turned his head, searching for a gap, but the wall stretched out as far as he could see.

If he wanted to get over it, they'd have to jump.

Matheus dug his heels deeper into Mungo's sides. The wall looked like it was about four feet tall. Could mules even jump that high?

The horses behind him grew even closer. He could almost feel their hot breath on his neck.

A few strides from the wall, Matheus squeezed Mungo as hard as he could and lifted himself off the mule's back. Without missing a beat, Mungo rocked onto his haunches and launched into the air, clearing the top of the wall by a few inches and landing in the water with a splash.

Matheus twisted around and saw the horses skid to a stop. One rider grabbed on to his mount's neck at the last minute. The other catapulted over his horse's head and tumbled down the muddy bank, landing with a groan.

Matheus gave Mungo a big pat and sent him forward, wading through the murky water. In the distance, the normally dark cityscape was dotted with clusters of light.

The mobs had stormed the city as well. It was only a matter of time before they attacked the cathedral.

He only hoped he wasn't too late.

By the time Mungo and Matheus entered the stable yard, they were both sopping wet and shivering. Yet Matheus could barely feel the cold.

He wasn't sure he'd be able to feel anything ever again.

Matheus dismounted and raced through the deserted courtyard. "They're coming," he yelled as he scrambled into the chapter house. "They're coming!" Although he could feel the force of the words in his throat, they barely seemed to make a sound. It was like hearing someone else shout from very far away.

A few of the other altar boys came running. "What's wrong?" Jan asked.

"Get the dean. Or the canon. Anyone," he panted.

"Matheus," Father Gerard said, stepping into the room. "Tell me what's going on."

"You!" Matheus found himself saying. "Get back." The altar boys' eyes widened, but he didn't care. Let them think he'd gone mad. "I know what you are."

"I assure you, whatever you think is wrong. Come with me."

"*No,*" Matheus spat, sensation returning to his body like a frostbitten limb removed from the cold. Except that all he could feel was hot rage. "Your *friends* are coming for the altarpiece, but I won't let them take it."

Father Gerard's face paled, but his expression remained calm. "Jan, run to the guard tower," the priest ordered another boy. "Tell them to send as many soldiers as they can. And then wait there until morning. It won't be safe to come back."

Jan stared at him for a moment, as if unsure whether the priest was being serious.

"Now!"

He took off at a sprint.

"Thomas, go lock all the doors. And secure the windows in the offices and your dormitory." Thomas didn't wait to be told twice.

"Getting rid of the altar boys won't help you," Matheus said. "I'm not going anywhere." He pushed past the priest into the corridor, and began running toward the sanctuary.

"Matheus!" Father Gerard shouted. He glanced over his shoulder and saw the priest sweeping toward him, his robes billowing behind him.

Matheus turned back around and sprinted down the center aisle. When he reached the altarpiece, he spun on his heel and stretched his arms out. "Stay back!" he shouted as Father Gerard reached for him.

"My son," he panted. "You misunderstand. I am not your enemy."

"Then what are you, *Father*? Are you even a real priest?"

The stern look on Father Gerard's face snuffed out the flames of Matheus's rage. "I am. I have committed my life to two purposes: serving God, and fighting those who seek to undo his work."

"The Vespers?" Matheus whispered. The priest nodded. "They're coming," Matheus continued. "They're coming for the altarpiece."

Father Gerard pressed his lips together and turned to face the paintings.

"What do they want with it?" Matheus asked. "The man — the Vesper — said something about a map."

The priest looked at Matheus, startled. "What do you know about that?"

Matheus felt his stomach lurch. "It was my mother, but she never had the chance . . . to explain." Father Gerard stared at Matheus for a moment. His features folded into comprehension, and he placed his hand on Matheus's shoulder. "I am so, so sorry, my child."

They were interrupted by the sound of stomping boots. Father Gerard and Matheus spun around and saw a line of soldiers marching down the aisle. Seeing their swords glittering in the candlelight was almost as incomprehensible as seeing the dagger in Mother's chest. Weapons did not belong in a church.

The captain stepped forward and removed his hat. "We've secured the entrances, Father," he said, bowing his head. "And I have men surrounding the perimeter."

Father Gerard nodded. "How long do you think we'll be able to hold them off?"

The captain shifted uncomfortably. "There are smaller mobs all over the city. They've been burning shops, breaking windows. If they keep going as they are, we'll be fine. But if they decide to band together . . ." He trailed off.

"If there's any chance of them gaining entry, we'll have to move the altarpiece," Father Gerard said briskly, and the soldiers' eyes widened.

"We can't risk moving it out of the cathedral tonight,

though," Father Gerard continued. "We'll have to dismantle the altarpiece and hide the paintings somewhere inside the building."

"How about the crypt?" called one of the soldiers.

"They'll look there."

"The kitchens?"

The priest shook his head.

This is useless, Matheus thought. What was the point of hiding the paintings? The Vespers wouldn't let the mob stop until they found them. They weren't going to leave empty-handed. If all the soldiers were in the cathedral, it would be hard to convince anyone that the altarpiece had gone elsewhere. Unless . . .

"Father," Matheus said, turning to the priest. "I have an idea."

Matheus sat on the stone steps that led up to the now-barren altar. He shivered as the damp from the stone seeped into the breeches that had barely had time to dry since he and Mungo had emerged from the canal.

The sanctuary was completely empty, save for him and Father Gerard. They'd overseen the soldiers as they dismantled the altarpiece and carried the paintings to the chosen hiding place.

Over the past hour, the noise outside had increased. What began as a smattering of shouts had grown into a frenzy of angry chants, stomps, and shrieks that filled the cathedral like chords from a demonic organ.

The number of torches had multiplied as well. The faint flickers behind the stained glass windows grew into flames, engulfing the figures in a shadowy blaze that could only have escaped from the depths of hell.

The crackle of burning wood grew louder, and Matheus could now smell the smoke drifting through the gaps in the windows. There'd been a number of bangs against the door—probably from men trying to kick it in—but it had held.

But then there was another sound at the door. A louder thud followed by an ominous *crack*.

"They've found a battering ram," Father Gerard said, rising from the step.

He turned to Matheus. "It's time. Are you ready?"

Matheus nodded, even though his frantic heart was trying to convey a different answer.

He squeezed Matheus's arm. "Good luck."

Matheus sprinted up the aisle and tore up the spiral staircase that led to the bell tower. A few steps from the top, he turned around and took a deep breath, running over the plan in his head.

There was another *crack*, followed by a chorus of shouts that echoed through the sanctuary and up into the tower. Matheus's whole body froze.

The clash of swords joined the cacophony of sounds that filled the cathedral. The soldiers must have started trying to drive the mob out. But it was clear they were outnumbered, because soon shouts were ringing from throughout the building.

"Check the crypt!" Matheus heard someone cry.

"They could've hidden it in the balcony."

"Look inside the pews!"

Sweat formed on Matheus's forehead as the noises grew louder. They were getting closer.

"Search the towers," a low voice commanded, setting Matheus's cheeks ablaze while his stomach churned.

It was the Vesper.

A ball of rage surged through him, incinerating every other feeling. His muscles were on fire. He felt like he could lift the altarpiece himself. He could fight off the intruders single-handedly.

He could slam the man into the cathedral wall until his body disintegrated into dust.

Matheus jumped down the steps onto the landing, his hands clenched into fists. But then another thought fluttered to the surface of his mind, like a phoenix rising out of the flames.

His job was to protect the altarpiece. His mother had given her life for it.

Matheus took a deep breath and returned to his spot on the step.

The shouts grew louder, punctuated by screams. Matheus closed his eyes, trying to focus on something other than the terrible scene playing out below. He thought about the main panel of the altarpiece. The green meadow sparkling in the dazzling sunlight. The snow-white lamb.

The sound of approaching footsteps echoed up the staircase.

That was his sign.

Matheus scrambled up the stairs, feeling the temperature change as he approached the top. He'd never been up here, as the bell tower was strictly off-limits. But now was not the time to worry about protocol.

He ducked under a low doorway, shivering as the night air swirled around him. The massive bells blocked almost all of the moon, but the sky was full of glittering stars. Matheus ducked under a wooden beam and took a few shaky steps along the narrow ledge. To his right was the chamber that housed the ropes and wheels that controlled the bell. To his left was a low stone wall, and beyond that, nothing. Anyone unfortunate enough to lose his balance would plummet nearly three hundred feet to the ground.

Against his better judgment, Matheus turned his head to look over the edge. Through the dizzying expanse of darkness, he could make out the flicker of flames on all sides. The cathedral was surrounded.

There was another burst of footsteps, followed by a series of shouts. At first, all he could see was a line of shadows gliding along the stone wall of the staircase. But then two figures careened around the bend, waving their torches through the dark air — the Vesper and another man in black.

Matheus scurried around to the other side of the

bell, praying that the shadows cast by the rafters would obscure his own. He fished the bits of cloth Father Gerard had given him out of his pocket, stuffed them in his ears until the world fell silent. Then he stood on his toes and reached for the heavy rope that hung from a hook on one of the beams.

Their shadows began sliding along the ledge. If they looked down into the bell chamber, they'd find what they were looking for. At Matheus's suggestion, the guards had dismantled the altarpiece and hidden the panels along the inside of the bell tower.

He unhooked the rope and held it tightly with both hands as he watched the men creep closer.

It was time.

Matheus took a deep breath, bent his knees, and pulled on the rope as hard as he could. There was a low *clank*, and suddenly, Matheus was yanked off his feet. He screamed and held on to the rope as he felt himself twisting in the air. Then another sound exploded through the tower as the bell began to ring. Matheus shut his eyes as the vibrations coursed through him, shaking every bone in his body. In the brief moment of reprieve, Matheus thought he could hear the Vespers screaming, but he wasn't sure.

The bell tolled again, and then again, sending new waves of sound pulsing through him. For a few moments, all that existed was the peal of the bell, as if the sky had opened up and God himself was shouting vengeance from the heavens.

Matheus opened his eyes and saw the men stumbling toward the door, their faces contorted in agony.

Soon, the twisting stopped, and he lowered himself back onto the ledge. His feet gave out and he fell onto the cold stone in a crumpled heap. He began to cry noiselessly. The ringing of the bell had silenced all other sounds in the world.

Early the next morning, Matheus stood at the top of the bell tower, helping Father Gerard oversee the removal of the altarpiece. The mob had finally dispersed, and the mayor of Ghent had agreed to let them keep the altarpiece in the fort until the city settled down.

After the last panel was safely removed, Matheus turned to watch the sun rising over the eastern edge of the city, casting a shimmering glow on the houses and flecking the river with sparks of gold light. It was hard to believe that only a few hours earlier, the torch flames had ripped open the night sky.

As he scanned the horizon, he tried to imagine the scene at his house. Was his mother still lying where she fell? Was the house even standing? Or had it been devoured by the hungry fire he'd seen spitting and hissing on the torches? He prayed that his father and baby Greet had emerged unscathed.

"You were very brave last night, Matheus," the priest said, placing his hand on the boy's shoulder.

"Thank you, Father." He supposed he should be proud, but all he felt was loss. The altarpiece was safe, but his mother was gone.

Father Gerard turned to look at him. "You may not understand it now, but you've done the world an enormous service. The Vespers are a dangerous force. If they had gotten hold of the altarpiece, they could have become even more powerful."

"Because of the map? What was that man even talking about? There's no map in any of the paintings."

"The Vespers believe that there are hidden symbols in the altarpiece that, when translated correctly, identify a number of secret locations around the world. Hiding places for something of great value."

Matheus tilted his head to the side. "A treasure?"

Father Gerard gave him a sad smile. "If only that were it."

Matheus closed his eyes as the terrible image he'd been struggling to banish took root in his mind. His mother lying on the floor. Whatever the Vespers were looking for, they couldn't be allowed to find it. Matheus would see to that.

A soft wind blew through the tower, and the air streaming across the bell created a whistling sound, like ghosts of last night's ringing. *No*, Matheus thought as he listened closer. *It sounds like a voice.* He could almost hear the bell whispering to him. He craned his head up to look at the brightening sky, and mouthed a silent good-bye.

PART 2

Massachusetts, 1945

Grace Cahill held the two envelopes in her hand: one beige, one light blue. She stared at them for a moment before crumpling the blue envelope into a ball and tossing it into the crackling fireplace — the one redeeming feature of the dreary senior common room at Miss Harper's School for Girls. It didn't matter that the blue letter had been sent all the way from Paris. She was done with all that.

That Grace Cahill didn't exist anymore.

All she cared about was the second envelope, which bore a US Army stamp and a label that read *Passed by Army Examiner.* Grace had received a few similar envelopes ever since her favorite teacher, Mr. Blythe, or rather, Captain Blythe, had joined the army. Although an old football injury had left him unfit for normal military service, the government had made an exception when they recruited for some top secret project involving stolen works of art. And so, three years after the

United States entered the Second World War, Mr. Blythe resigned from his art history post and shipped overseas.

Grace slid her finger under the seal and carefully opened the envelope. The letter inside was scribbled on very thin stationery, and there were all sorts of stains and fingerprints around the edges from the censor assigned to screen it for security breaches. Grace trembled as she ran her finger over the wrinkled paper. It almost seemed to have battle scars of its own.

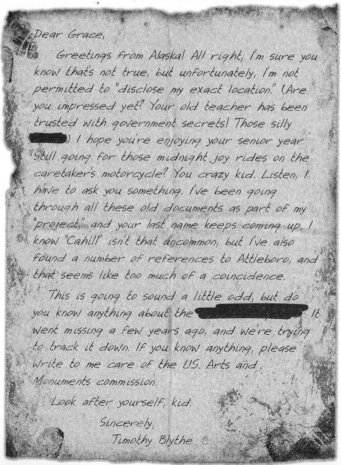

Dear Grace,

Greetings from Alaska! All right, I'm sure you know that's not true, but unfortunately, I'm not permitted to "disclose my exact location." (Are you impressed yet? Your old teacher has been trusted with government secrets! Those silly ████) I hope you're enjoying your senior year. Still going for those midnight joy rides on the caretaker's motorcycle? You crazy kid. Listen, I have to ask you something. I've been going through all these old documents as part of my "project," and your last name keeps coming up. I know "Cahill" isn't that uncommon, but I've also found a number of references to Attleboro, and that seems like too much of a coincidence.

This is going to sound a little odd, but do you know anything about the ████████████? It went missing a few years ago, and we're trying to track it down. If you know anything, please write to me care of the U.S. Arts and Monuments commission.

Look after yourself, kid.

Sincerely,
Timothy Blythe

Grace grasped the arm of the couch as the room began to spin. She tried to force herself to breathe, but her chest seemed to be tightening, collapsing the space between her rib cage and her heart.

It wasn't just the shock of seeing Mr. Blythe's distinct handwriting. It wasn't fear that the army was unearthing her family's deepest secrets.

It was because Mr. Blythe was dead.

Grace leaned back against the couch, oblivious to the metal springs jabbing her spine.

Three weeks ago, during morning convocation, the headmistress had made the grave announcement. "I regret to inform you," she'd said stiffly, "that Mr. Blythe was killed in action during a secret operation in Germany." She placed the emphasis on odd words, like an actor reading a script for the first time, and for a moment, the meaning hung in the air. But then the chapel filled with the wails of girls — some genuinely distraught, some exaggerating their grief for the young, well-liked teacher.

Unlike the other faculty members at Miss Harper's School, who doubted whether girls really needed to know much more than etiquette and dancing, Mr. Blythe had considered it his job to challenge his students. He'd taken a special interest in Grace and told her she was destined for "great things."

He had no idea.

By the time she'd met Mr. Blythe, Grace had already flown a plane into the middle of a battle. She'd even found one of the 39 Clues that her family — some of the most powerful people in history — had spent centuries looking for.

It'd been easy to risk her life when she thought she was protecting the Clues from the power-hungry Cahill branches, or the mysterious Vespers. But over the past year, as news from Europe came streaming in through somber radio reports, chilling newspaper photos, and casualty lists, an unsettling realization began to fray the edges of her fantasy. The Cahills weren't saving the world — they were going on an insane treasure hunt while the world burned around them.

This was why Grace had been ignoring the blue envelopes. They were from a Cahill at the Louvre museum in Paris, who wanted Grace's help tracking down a painting — something to do with the Clues, no doubt. A year ago, she would have been intrigued by the challenge, but now the thought made her ill. She could only imagine the ways her more ruthless relatives had found to exploit a war that had already claimed millions of lives.

She glanced down at the letter and felt her stomach twist.

And now one more.

Grace ran her finger over the paper. Mr. Blythe must have written it a few days before he died. The envelope had traversed the war-ravaged landscape, avoiding bombs and bullets, in order to find its way to her.

It had survived, while the man who had written it had not.

She folded it in half carefully and tucked it into her bag. The war might not have stopped the Cahills, but they would have to carry on without her.

She was done.

By the time she arrived at the lecture hall, everyone else was seated. Grace had just slid into a seat by the door when Miss Harper, the headmistress, swept inside, followed by a woman she'd never seen before.

There was a faint rustling as the students hurried to straighten their papers, smooth their hair, and readjust their skirts so the hems draped gracefully over their knees. The headmistress cleared her throat. "Mrs. Prentice has taken ill and will be unable to teach for the rest of the semester."

That was odd. Just yesterday, Grace had walked past the faculty lounge and caught a glimpse of the sprightly Mrs. Prentice showing the chemistry teacher how to foxtrot. She certainly hadn't seemed ill then.

"Fortunately, we were able to find a wonderful substitute, Mademoiselle Hubert." The headmistress pronounced the name "Oo-*bear*," contorting her mouth as if forcing her reluctant lips to wrap around the foreign-sounding syllables. "She recently arrived from Paris to study . . ." She glanced at Mlle Hubert.

"Nineteenth-century American painting," the other woman said, her French accent coating the words like a glossy veneer. "I spend most of my time in Boston, but I am happy for the chance to teach a few days a week."

Grace had trouble believing that Mlle Hubert harbored a deep desire to teach. With her sleek bobbed hair, dark red lips, and elegantly tailored suit, she looked like she should be posing for a photographer in front of the Eiffel Tower instead of locked in a musty classroom, trying in vain to convince Mary Atkinson that Monet and Manet were two different people.

However, that wasn't the only reason Grace had trouble taking her eyes off Mlle Hubert. She looked vaguely familiar, yet Grace couldn't remember where she'd seen her. Perhaps their paths had crossed at one of the Boston museums. Over the past few years, she'd spent a good deal of her free time wandering around the Museum of Fine Arts. She'd even taken her little brother, Fiske, with her a few times. Although he'd never get to meet their mother, Grace could show him the paintings that had meant so much to Edith. Grace knew it was silly, but it was a comfort to drink in the same images her mother had loved.

"Lovely," the headmistress said quickly. She clasped her hands and smiled at the class. "I suppose that's all. Be good for Mlle Hubert, girls," she said as she headed toward the door.

"Well then," Mlle Hubert said, addressing the students. She smiled, and the corners of her ruby lips spread across her pale cheeks like a ribbon of blood. "Today, we discuss the Northern European Renaissance."

Arlene Swenson, a nervous-looking girl with shortly cropped curly hair, raised her hand. Mlle Hubert nodded at her. "Yes?"

"We've been studying the Impressionists, miss—" Mlle Hubert raised her eyebrow. "I mean, *mademoiselle*."

"Bah. I cannot stand zee Impressionists." Mlle Hubert waved her hand dismissively. "All those silly dots." She took a breath. "*Non*. The Renaissance painters were the *real* masters. I show you." She sauntered over to the wall, switched off the lights, and slipped a slide into the projector. An image of a dour-looking man in a floppy black hat flashed onto the screen at the front of the classroom. "*Voilà*. Here we have very important work . . . erm, 'Man in Hat.'"

Arlene cleared her throat. "Excuse me, mademoiselle, but isn't that Rembrandt's self-portrait?"

"Ah, yes, that is the more . . . *colloquial* title."

She switched slides and a new painting appeared—a richly colored Madonna and child. "And another . . . very famous . . . masterpiece. 'Lady in Long Dress.'"

"Hold on. Isn't that—"

Mlle Hubert changed the slide before Arlene had a chance to speak.

"Wait!" Isabel Faust called out. "Can you go back? I didn't get to finish my notes."

"No time," Mlle Hubert said brusquely. "We have much to do." The next slide appeared, a chilling depiction of Christ's crucifixion. "How charming." She clicked through the next four paintings so quickly Grace didn't have time to register what they were.

"Ah, here we are," Mlle Hubert said, as a new image filled the screen.

Grace inhaled sharply as a flood of long-forgotten memories swept through her. It was "The Adoration of the Mystic Lamb," Jan van Eyck's masterpiece, and her mother's favorite work of art.

"Sadly, the altarpiece disappeared a few years after the start of the war." Mlle Hubert's voice pulled Grace back from her thoughts.

"How can something that size disappear?" Arlene asked, a hint of skepticism coloring her tone.

"It is a tragic story." The teacher sighed dramatically. "After the war began, the altarpiece was brought from Belgium to France for safekeeping. The director of the Louvre had arranged for important pieces to be hidden throughout the country, away from the fighting. But the 'Lamb' was seized by the Germans and has not been seen since."

Although the crowded classroom was stuffy and warm, a chill passed over Grace. It was like hearing someone had died. She knew it was silly—the people in the paintings weren't alive. They didn't care whether they stood in the sun-drenched cathedral or in the dank basement of some Nazi art thief.

The altarpiece was another casualty of war, just like Mr. Blythe.

Grace tried to put it out of her mind, but an idea had formed that she couldn't uproot.

The altarpiece had been in the Louvre's care when it went missing. The woman writing her from Paris—Rose Valland—worked for the Louvre. Could *that* be what she wanted Grace to find? She instinctively reached into her bag to run her fingers along the edge of Mr. Blythe's letter. His section was in charge of tracking down missing works of art. A wave of nausea passed over her. Had he been looking for the "Lamb" as well?

Grace held on to the edge of the desk as the room began to spin. For centuries, the Cahills had been using the military for their own purposes. Napoleon sent the French army to invade Egypt to help him find a lost Clue. What if Mr. Blythe's department had been set up by Cahills searching for the altarpiece?

We could be the ones who sent him into danger.

We killed him.

"Ahem." She looked up and saw Mlle Hubert staring at her.

Grace swallowed, trying to suppress the bile rising up from her stomach. "Can you repeat the question?"

The teacher pursed her red lips. "I was explaining that Van Eyck hid a number of messages in the work, and I was hoping that you would be so kind as to locate one on the slide."

The other girls all turned to stare at Grace, but her eyes were automatically drawn toward one of the figures in the background. She knew that there were Hebrew letters painted onto the band of his hat, but something about Mlle Hubert's expression made her hesitant to mention it aloud.

"I'm not sure . . . sorry."

A flash of irritation crossed Mlle Hubert's face. "You look at one of the most beautiful, complex works of art in the world and think nothing? *C'est dommage.*" Mlle Hubert shook her head. "Perhaps you are more interested in whatever is in your bag?"

Grace glanced down and saw that her hand was still inside her satchel. She snatched it back and placed both hands in her lap. "No, mademoiselle."

The teacher took a step forward and extended her smooth, slender arm. "Give it to me."

"It's nothing."

"I am not going to ask you again."

Grace reached into her bag and removed the envelope, the sweat from her palm seeping into the paper.

The clack of Mlle Hubert's high heels echoed through the room as she strode toward Grace and snatched the letter out of her hand. "From a boy, I assume?" She smirked. "It is best that I take it. You obviously cannot afford to be distracted from your studies."

As Mlle Hubert sauntered back toward the projector, Grace felt a fresh wave of grief pass over her. But then her pain hardened into anger. She might not have been able to save Mr. Blythe, but she could certainly save his last letter.

Mlle Oo-bear had no idea who she was dealing with.

Grace hit the ground silently. It had been six months since she'd gone for a midnight training run — six months since she'd resolved that her days as a Madrigal agent were over. But she hadn't lost her knack for balancing on the sill, leaping for the tree branch, and then dropping lightly onto the spongy grass below.

She wasn't going to allow Mr. Blythe's last letter to molder away like some forgotten prisoner.

She was going to get it back.

Grace jogged across the lawn toward the back gate, passing Kendrick Hall, the ivy-covered building that housed the teachers' offices. A light on the second floor caught her eye and a dark figure passed in front of the glowing window. Grace recognized the elegant silhouette.

It was Mlle Hubert.

Grace ducked behind a tree.

The window went dark, and Grace exhaled with relief. A minute later, a figure emerged from the building and hurried down the path, away from Grace.

When Mlle Hubert disappeared from sight, Grace darted out from behind the tree and ran up to the front door of Kendrick Hall. She turned the handle. It was locked. With a quick glance over her shoulder, Grace dashed around to the side of the building. She stood there for a moment with her back pressed up against cold brick.

She surveyed the lawn one more time, then turned around. The large bricks were old and uneven, which made it easy to find a foothold and hoist herself off the ground. Grace reached up, feeling the bricks for more cracks, and pulled herself even higher. A gust of wind rushed by, twisting the hem of her dress around her calves. Grace tightened her grip and shook her legs free one at a time. After flying an airplane into the middle of a raging battle and dodging bullets in the Tower of London, sneaking into a second-floor office was a piece of cake.

Grace rested her knee on the windowsill, braced one arm against the wall, and pulled up on the sash. It was unlocked. She lowered herself onto the floor, wrinkling her nose. Mlle Hubert had only been here one day, and already the room had changed. Mrs. Prentice's office had always smelled like coffee and gingersnaps, but now the still air was saturated with the scent of perfume and cigarettes.

The room was dark, but the dim moonlight that filtered through the glass provided just enough illumination to poke around. Grace crept over toward the desk, scanning the jumble of papers, books, ashtrays, and teacups with red lipstick stains on the rims, but the envelope was nowhere to be seen.

A noise from downstairs sent Grace diving under the desk. She couldn't afford to be caught breaking into a teacher's office. Her father had warned her that she was one suspension away from being sent to live with distant relatives in Siberia. Not that the school would even be able to get hold of James Cahill if they caught her. Last she heard, he was in Brazil. Or was it Finland?

Grace tucked her legs in and braced for the sound of approaching footsteps. But none came. Sighing, she leaned back against the table leg and winced as something dug into the space between her shoulder blades. Grace twisted around and saw a raised seam running partway down the leg of the desk, as if a section had been replaced. She ran her finger along the edge, feeling it wiggle slightly, then dug her nails under the seam and pulled. A chunk of wood slid out, revealing a cylinder of tightly rolled paper.

Grace crept out from under the desk to where there was slightly more light, ignoring the thud of her heart against her chest. Had Mrs. Prentice done this? Or had her replacement been redecorating?

She removed the top paper and spread it out on the floor, holding the edges down to keep it flat.

It was a telegram sent from Berlin to Paris, dated a few weeks back. But it wasn't written in any language she recognized. Certainly not German or French. She lowered her head for a closer look. The letters were all familiar — it was just the order that didn't make sense. It almost looked like a code, but what sort of art history teacher was in the habit of hiding encrypted messages?

She ignored the prickle of fear in her stomach. There was no reason to jump to conclusions.

Not until she cracked the code.

Grace stood up and rummaged through the desk clutter for a pencil and a piece of paper. The message looked like it could be a substitution cipher, and since the letter V showed up a number of times on its own, that meant it probably stood for either I or A. If V stood for I, then it made sense that W would stand for J and so on. She started to scribble, her brow furrowing as a stream of nonsense appeared. She crossed it out and tried again, this time, with V standing in for A.

This time, the words looked familiar. The message was written in French! Grace knew the language well enough to translate.

Hubert —

We have the altarpiece, but need more time. Most of our enemies have been eliminated, but we cannot take any chances. Go to Massachusetts and take care of the Cahill girl. She made a mess of things in Morocco, and must not be allowed to interfere again. I have arranged to remove her art history teacher. Find out what Grace knows before you kill her.

— Vesper Four

Grace stared at her hastily transcribed message. If she waited long enough, perhaps the letters would rearrange themselves into words that made sense, that didn't make her feel like she was free-falling.

The Vespers had the altarpiece. They knew she was

being recruited to rescue it. And so they'd sent one of their agents to kill her.

It was one thing to fight for her life on a mission, when she'd knowingly rushed headlong into danger. But here? At *school*? She grabbed on to the desk to steady herself as her knees began to tremble.

Grace stuffed the telegram into her pocket and turned back toward the window. She tried to hurry, but her legs felt like they were made of lead. She took a deep breath, coughing as a cloud of French perfume filled her lungs.

"Good evening." Grace spun around quickly, and slipped on the edge of the thin carpet, landing with a hard thud on the floor. She rolled over and looked up.

Mlle Hubert was leaning against the door, one hand resting casually on her hip.

The other holding a knife.

"I cannot decide whether you are much more intelligent than I supposed, or just much—what is the word?—more nose? Nosier." She was looking at Grace with a combination of fascination and disgust. "But of course, that is what you Madrigals do."

Grace rose shakily to her feet, cursing herself for not making it to the window in time. This is what happened when you stopped training. "So you're here to kill me?" Grace asked, forcing her voice to assume a slightly condescending tone. She gave Mlle Hubert the same smile she'd seen her cousin Princess Elizabeth give young men who tried to impress her at royal gatherings. "They'll find out. And I think you'll find the éclairs in federal prison aren't quite up to your standard."

Mlle Hubert snorted. "That will not be a problem." She held the knife up in the air so it glinted faintly in the moonlight. "Disposing of the body is the easy part." She tilted the weapon to the side, as if it were a bracelet she was considering in a shop. "But that might not be necessary, if you decide to be cooperative." She turned to Grace. "What do you know about the Ghent altarpiece?"

"Nothing," she said quickly.

Mlle Hubert raised an eyebrow. "Then why was that teacher writing to you about it?"

Grace's stomach twisted at the thought of the vile woman reading her letter, but she kept her face impassive. "He didn't say anything about the altarpiece."

"The actual name was censored, of course," Mlle Hubert said, rolling her eyes. "But I know that is the work he was referring to. That is what he was sent to Germany to find." She smirked. "That is why we had to kill him."

Grace felt her heart speed up. "The Germans killed him."

"The order came from a Vesper officer."

"You're working with the *Nazis*?" Grace spat.

Mlle Hubert smiled. "They are very good at

carrying out orders. I think it only took one bullet to kill poor Mr. Blythe."

It was as if someone had ignited a set of rockets attached to Grace's feet. She launched herself at Mlle Hubert, wrestling her to the floor. She rolled on top of her and was about to deliver another blow when she felt something cold and sharp pressed against her neck. Grace lowered her eyes slowly. Mlle Hubert had the point of the knife digging into her throat. "Get up," she said icily.

Grace hesitated, and her body grew rigid. She considered trying to knock the knife out of Mlle Hubert's hand but, as she tensed her shoulder to make her move, the blade went deeper. Grace yelped.

"*Quiet!*" Mlle Hubert hissed. "Get up, *now.*"

She rose shakily to her feet and took a few steps back toward the door, but Mlle Hubert had risen quickly and was already standing in front of her, pressing the edge of the knife against the side of Grace's neck.

"I am only going to ask you once more. What do you know about the altarpiece?"

Grace's mind began to race as she desperately tried to recall everything her mother had told her about the "Lamb." "There are hidden Hebrew letters on one of the figures' hats," she said quickly, feeling the blade rise and fall as she spoke.

Mlle Hubert pressed the knife deeper. "Everyone knows that."

Grace's heart was pounding, urging her brain to

work faster. "One of the panels is a reproduction."

"I know. *We* stole the original." She pushed on the blade even harder.

"Van Eyck was a secret agent!" Grace gagged, fighting to speak as the knife pressed against her windpipe. That was something she remembered her mother telling her. "He was sent . . . by the Duke of Burgundy . . . to spy on other courts."

"Yes," Mlle Hubert snapped. "Which is why we want to know what secret information he hid in the paintings." She lowered the knife and stepped to the side.

Grace gasped and brought her hand to her neck, wiping away the blood that had begun to trickle down toward her collar.

"I am done wasting my time," Mlle Hubert said. "Max!" she shouted. A figure appeared in the doorway. An enormous man wearing a long coat . . . and holding a gun.

"Miss Cahill is not in the mood for conversation. Let us make sure she never has to make small talk again."

The man raised his arm so the barrel of the gun pointed right between Grace's eyes.

Grace leaped to the side the same moment the gun exploded. A bullet ricocheted off the wall next to Grace's left ear, filling her head with a nauseating ring. She hurtled toward the window, and hoisted herself onto the ledge. There was another crack as a bullet hit the panes, showering Grace with tiny shards of broken glass. There was no time to climb down. She'd have to jump.

Grace twisted around so her feet were pointed toward the ground, took a quick breath, and let go, her arms flailing as she grasped at the empty night air.

She hit the ground with a thud and rolled a few feet. Everything hurt. But before she could assess the specific damage, the gunshots began again. Grace began crawling away from the building, shrieking as a bullet flew right past her cheek. The shooting stopped, and Grace knew that Mlle Hubert and the other Vesper were on their way downstairs. She had to get away. Grace rose to her feet, gasping as pain shot up her left leg.

"Help!" she screamed. "Somebody!"

She knew the dorms were too far away for anyone there to hear her, but there had to be someone around. A janitor. A teacher returning from a late night out. Anyone.

"Help!" she shouted again. But there was no answer. Her desperate scream was simply absorbed by the silence of the night.

She stumbled down the path toward the staff garage, gasping at the pain. Before she gave up training, she used to "borrow" the groundskeeper's motorcycle for stomach-churning rides down twisty backcountry lanes. She prayed that it was still there.

She could hear footsteps behind her. Grace frantically grabbed the dead bolt and threw open the wooden doors. The garage was mostly empty, but she felt a wave of joy rush over her as she spotted the caretaker's motorcycle leaning against the wall—just where she'd found it the last time she'd taken it.

Balancing on her uninjured right leg, Grace flung herself into the seat, stuck the key into the ignition, and kicked the motor over to start. The engine rumbled to life. She pressed the gas, shooting out of the garage like a rocket.

Mlle Hubert and her assassin were running down the path toward her.

"Kill her!" her teacher screamed, as Grace picked up speed.

The man raised his gun, but Grace leaned forward, hugging the motorcycle as the bullets flew over her back.

"The tires, you idiot," Mlle Hubert shrieked. But it was too late. Grace sped past them, creating a rush of wind that blew Mlle Hubert's scarf over her face. The front gate was open slightly. The Vesper must not have locked it when he sneaked into the school. Grace switched into a higher gear as she flew through the narrow gap and onto the road.

"Woo-hoo!" she shouted as she raced down the

middle of the empty street, her hair streaming behind her.

It didn't matter that, with every bump, her left ankle screamed in protest.

She was alive.

It was almost dawn by the time Grace coasted into the Boston Navy Yard. Set against the pink and orange sky, the enormous warships looked like they were emerging from another world. Grace shivered as she imagined them being forged by giants, sent to Earth to battle the evil that threatened to destroy it.

It had been foolish to ignore all those letters from the woman at the Louvre. No, not just foolish. Selfish. Reckless. And fatal. If she'd only acted earlier, perhaps *she* could have found the altarpiece. Mr. Blythe might have never been sent to Germany. He would never have been struck by a Vesper bullet.

It had been ridiculous to think that she could remove herself from the Clue hunt, separate herself from the Cahills' centuries-old feud with a ruthless enemy. Growing up, she had always associated the word *Vesper* with evil, but it had been an abstract evil — like the villain in a fairy tale. Over the past few years, Grace, along with the rest of the world, had seen real evil. Or at least they'd heard about it, listening to seasoned radio announcers who couldn't mask the horror in their voices as they reported on Nazi atrocities. They'd read about it, in newspaper articles about what soldiers discovered after they liberated the concentration camps.

A photograph of the prisoners flashed through her mind. The worn faces that looked like all life had been drained out of them, leaving hollow eyes and sunken cheeks like dry riverbeds after a drought. The thought of the perpetrators made Grace physically ill.

They were who the Vespers had chosen to do their dirty work?

She didn't know what the Vespers wanted, but until they found it, innocent people would continue to die.

Unless the Cahills destroyed them first.

Commercial steam liners weren't crossing the Atlantic. The only way to Europe was aboard a military ship or plane, and they didn't sell tickets.

Grace knew what she had to do.

She leaned the motorcycle against a wall and covered it with a dirty tarp. Then, with a glance over her shoulder, she darted to the edge of a dock where navy workers were loading supplies onto one of the ships.

Grace slipped into the narrow space between the tall columns of crates and held on tight as the platform was hauled into the air.

A few minutes later, there was a loud *bang*, and everything went dark as the crate was loaded into what she assumed was the hull of the ship.

It was going to be a very, very long trip to France.

The first time Grace had crossed the Atlantic, it had been on a luxury ocean liner, where she'd spent the afternoons sipping tea in the parlor, and the evenings listening to a jazz trio play under a canopy of stars.

The stars probably hadn't changed, but she was in no position to marvel at them.

Grace wasn't even sure how long she spent in the cargo hold. There weren't any windows, so she couldn't keep track of the sunrises, and there wasn't enough light for her to read her watch. For three or four days, she huddled on the cold floor, nibbling at the biscuits she'd unearthed from one of the crates, drinking from a fire hose she'd found coiled up in a corner.

If Beatrice could only see me now, she thought grimly, imagining what her snooty older sister would say about these accommodations. Beatrice would never stow away on a navy ship. She'd made it clear that she wanted nothing to do with their family's secrets.

But Grace knew that was no longer an option for her. The Cahills had an obligation to do whatever they could to keep innocent people safe from the Vespers.

Her next stop would be the Louvre in Paris. She'd find out why that woman, Rose Valland, had needed her help, and what her plan was for retrieving the altarpiece.

She only hoped it wasn't too late.

Grace awoke from her nap with a jolt as the crates rattled around her. In the distance, she could make out the sound of men shouting, and felt a current of excitement travel down her aching limbs. They had arrived in Normandy, in northern France.

Grace took a few shaky steps forward and peered around a stack of metal containers. She had to figure out how to get off the ship without being spotted. Even seventeen-year-old girls couldn't get away with sneaking aboard a US Navy ship during wartime. She'd be lucky if she weren't shot on sight.

She crept down a deserted corridor lined with small, round windows filled with hazy sky and blue-gray water. A strange mix of awe and sadness churned her stomach as she saw the ships scattered along the coast. It was the same beach the forces had landed on nearly a year ago on D-Day, the massive offensive that had allowed the Allies to gain control of crucial territory in northern France. She remembered the footage from the newsreels. The men storming up from the waves by the thousands, barreling into enemy fire. A staggering number of lives had been lost, but their sacrifice had not been in vain. The Germans had retreated.

Now it was Grace's turn—to make sure Mr. Blythe's sacrifice hadn't been in vain.

She reached the end of the corridor and pressed her ear against a metal door. When she was sure no one was on the other side, Grace turned the handle and stepped into the light. She winced and held her hand up to her forehead to shield her eyes.

"Hey!" a man's voice shouted.

Grace jumped like she'd been electrocuted.

"What in God's name are you doing?"

Still half-blind, Grace spun around and started running.

"Come back here!"

Grace sprinted with all her might, but she was weak and woozy from her days in the cargo hold.

"Intruder!"

The thud of footsteps behind her exploded into a chorus of stomping feet and shouting voices.

Up ahead, there was a gap in the railing where a ramp met the deck. She took a sharp right and tore down the slippery incline.

"I got her!"

Grace felt fingers graze against her arm. She gasped and tried to pick up speed, but she had nothing left.

She was about halfway down the ramp, and the water loomed below her. Was it a twenty-foot drop? Thirty?

With her legs about to give out, Grace used her last ounce of strength to hurl herself over the railing. She forced her burning lungs to take one final gulp of air before her feet hit the water, and she plunged into the murky darkness.

Nine hours later, Grace was in the most beautiful city in the world, but neither the Eiffel Tower nor Notre Dame held any interest for her. All Grace could think about was how much her feet ached and how ridiculous she must look trudging across Paris in mud-splattered clothes that reeked of gasoline and salt water.

However, as she walked along the Seine toward the Louvre, Grace felt her black mood dissipating in the afternoon sunshine. She hadn't been in Paris during the German occupation, but it was clear that the city was reveling in its freedom—delighting in its first spring since the liberation. The sound of children laughing danced down the cobble-stoned streets, young women in brightly colored clothes shot coquettish glances at the soldiers resting in the grass, and the sidewalk cafés buzzed with animated chatter.

It was hard to believe that, only a short time ago, German tanks had patrolled the streets and banners emblazoned with swastikas adorned many of the buildings. Paris was living proof that the tide of war had turned: The Germans were retreating.

Grace's stomach rumbled as she passed a pâtisserie with a window full of pastel-colored macaroons, but now wasn't the time to stop for a snack. As she crossed the Pont des Arts and the Louvre came into view, Grace forgot about her stomach. She'd been to Paris a number of times growing up, but was always astonished by the size, beauty, and grandeur of the magnificent Renaissance palace. Its three enormous wings surrounded a vast courtyard that Grace couldn't look at without imagining it full of carriages and ladies with powdered wigs.

Grace dusted off her dirty skirt as best she could before marching into the entrance hall. She wasn't in the ideal outfit for requesting an interview with one of the curators, but it would have to do. She raised her chin just like she'd seen her mother do before voicing her opinion to one of the many ambassadors who used to come to their house for dinner.

Grace walked toward the information desk, the clack of her shoes echoing throughout the nearly empty vestibule. The woman behind the desk was filing her nails. When she heard Grace enter, she set the emery board down and looked up in surprise, but her expression quickly transformed into disgust.

"Est-ce que je vous aide?" she said, wrinkling her nose.

Grace cleared her throat. *"Bonjour. Je voudrais un rendez-vous avec Madame Valland."*

The receptionist stared at Grace as if she'd requested an audience with the president. "You are American, no?" Grace nodded. "Did you *swim* here?"

Grace raised her chin. "Yes. The North Atlantic is lovely this time of year. Especially now that the Germans have retreated. *You're welcome*, by the way."

The woman sniffed. "And what is your business with Madame Valland?"

"It's private and confidential."

"Well, you will have to make an appointment. Madame Valland is very busy."

"I assure you, she's been expecting me."

The receptionist raised an eyebrow. "Rose Valland is the associate curator of the most famous museum in the world. She is far too busy to entertain American tourists . . . street urchins . . ." She waved her hand. "Whatever you are."

Grace smiled benignly. "So busy that I imagine she doesn't post her own letters."

"I handle all of Madame Valland's correspondence."

"Then you are aware, no doubt, that she's been writing to a Grace Cahill care of Miss Harper's School in Massachusetts?"

She narrowed her eyes. "How do you know that?"

"*I* am Grace Cahill."

The receptionist stared at her for a moment and stood up. "I see. In that case, I will show you to her office . . . mademoiselle."

"Don't bother. I wouldn't want to take you away from what appear to be very important duties."

The woman flushed. "Fourth floor. Take that staircase there." She pointed.

Grace smiled. "*Merci.*"

Unlike the cheerful scenes she'd passed outside, the Louvre still bore the hallmarks of war. As Grace reached the fourth floor, she found herself in a corridor lined with ornate gold frames, the kind used to display the works of old masters like Raphael and Rembrandt. Except that the frames were empty. In place of canvases, their titles were scrawled in chalk on the walls. She shivered, overcome with a chill that had nothing to do with the drafts blowing through the cavernous galleries. It was like walking through a graveyard and recognizing the names on the tombstones.

She opened a small door that said ADMINISTRATION and entered a long hallway. Halfway down, she saw a door with the name VALLAND. It was open.

Grace paused. She'd been so focused on making it to Paris that she hadn't thought about what she would say when she arrived. "Sorry I ignored all your letters"? "I couldn't miss field hockey practice"? "I was convinced my family is evil but now I know the Vespers are worse so here I am"?

She took a deep breath and knocked on the door.

"*Entrez,*" a voice called.

Grace stepped inside the office. An older woman with dark, elegantly arranged hair was sitting behind an enormous claw-footed desk. Books and prints covered every surface. Tall stacks teetered precariously from the desk and chairs, and there were piles of documents scattered on the floor. Yet, despite the clutter, the office didn't seem messy or disorganized. In her navy blue suit, the woman behind the desk radiated calm and authority.

Grace cleared her throat. "I'm Grace Cahill. I believe you've been expecting me."

Rose Valland stared at her for what felt like a full minute, taking in Grace's matted hair and stained clothes. Then her face broke out into a smile. "Well, this is a surprise." She gestured to the one empty seat. "Please, sit down." As Grace arranged herself in the threadbare armchair, Rose stood up to retrieve a tea tray balanced on the edge of a crowded end table and brought it over to the desk. "Tea?" Grace nodded and was handed a delicate white cup decorated with blue flowers.

"I'm sorry I didn't write back," Grace said. She clutched the teacup, savoring the warmth she felt seeping into her skin.

"I understand," Rose said, taking a sip of tea and then returning the cup to the saucer. "The war has been difficult for all of us." Grace tilted her head down, so Rose wouldn't see the blush spreading over her cheeks. She'd spent most of the past few years safe and sound in America, far away from the fighting.

But she was here now.

She raised her chin. "I assume you want me to find the altarpiece."

Rose looked startled. "How did you know? I didn't mention the name in my letters. It was too dangerous."

Rose's face grew pale as Grace told her about Mr. Blythe and Mlle Hubert. "But why do they want the altarpiece?" Grace asked, taking a moment to sip her tea.

Rose walked over to one of the piles and picked up a large book resting on the top. She brought it over to the desk and sat back down in her chair. "Well," she said, opening it to a spread featuring the Ghent altarpiece. "Scholars have always been fascinated by the elements that suggest Van Eyck traveled far beyond Europe." She pointed to a cluster of palm trees so lifelike they looked as if they were about to begin swaying in the breeze. "How could a man who supposedly spent his whole life in Belgium paint palm trees without seeing them?"

Rose moved her finger over to a classical statue in the corner of another panel. "And this. It is almost a perfect reproduction of a Donatello piece in Italy. You have to remember that in Van Eyck's day, books were extremely rare. It is not as if he could have seen a painting of Donatello's sculpture. The incredible accuracy suggests that he went on journeys—trips he chose not to document." She looked up at Grace. "The Vespers believe the panels conceal a map that leads to secret locations in all the places Van Eyck visited."

"What are they looking for?"

"We're not sure." Her lips pressed together and her face turned serious. "But it's something important enough they're willing to kill for it." She placed her hand on Grace's shoulder. "Come with me."

Grace followed Rose through the deserted galleries. As they passed countless empty picture frames, Rose explained that the Nazis had been seizing priceless works of art since the war began, but the altarpiece had held a particular fascination. "The 'Lamb' has been a symbol of many things for many people," she said as they swept down a marble staircase. "Over the centuries, it has been claimed by rulers who saw it as a mark of prestige. Others—even non-Cahills—believed that it hides the key to a priceless treasure. Hitler is convinced one of the panels contains a map to the crown of thorns Christ wore during his crucifixion, which supposedly has supernatural powers." She gave Grace a wry smile. "That's probably why it was so easy for the Vespers to convince him to track it down."

They turned into a cavernous sculpture gallery. In the dim light, the few remaining statues cast long shadows, making it look like the empty pedestals were haunted by the ghosts of their missing occupants.

"So we need to find the altarpiece before the Vespers decode the map?" Grace asked, running her hand along the top of an empty pedestal where, according to the chalk markings, a Greek statue of Athena once rested. "And I'm part of the rescue team?"

Rose shook her head. "Your friend Mr. Blythe's division—the Monuments Men—think they've located the storehouse where the Germans have been hiding the stolen works of art."

"So what do you need me for?" Grace said, her voice rising with frustration.

Rose ignored her tone and continued calmly. "The Germans are monitoring the Monuments Men. We believe they have orders to demolish the storehouse if the Allies get too close. They would rather destroy thousands of European masterpieces than hand over their stolen treasures."

Grace narrowed her eyes. "How do you even know this?"

Rose walked over to a large ceramic urn. She glanced over her shoulder, grabbed on to the handle, and pulled.

Instead of the *smash* Grace expected, she heard the *clank* of twisting gears. The urn began to rotate, sinking down into the concrete pedestal until it disappeared completely, revealing an empty compartment. Rose reached in, pulled out a folder, and beckoned for Grace to stand next to her. She removed a stack of documents: letters and telegrams in a variety of languages.

Grace gasped as she glimpsed a black eagle clutching a swastika. "How did you get that?" she whispered.

Rose smiled. "Because, dear, I am not just a Madrigal. I'm also a member of the French Resistance."

Grace wandered through the empty gallery in a daze. She couldn't believe she'd agreed to this. Rose wanted her to *stall* the Nazis — to keep the altarpiece safe until the Monuments Men arrived. Because if the "Lamb" were destroyed before the Cahills decoded the map, they'd lose their one chance to discover what the Vespers were after.

Grace knew why saving the altarpiece was important, but the plan—if you could even call it that—was insane. In order to reach the "Lamb," Grace would have to sneak into the heart of Nazi-occupied Europe. The thought of getting into Austria was sheer madness. Exploring Altaussee—the town Rose identified—was tantamount to a suicide mission.

Rose told Grace that she knew someone who might be willing to fly her to Austria—a contact from the French Resistance. Their code of secrecy prevented Rose from calling her while Grace was in the room, and she politely requested that she wait in the gallery.

The museum was so quiet that Grace could make out the sound of a radio broadcast coming from one of the nearby offices. The familiar cadences settled in her ear and sent a shiver down her spine. It was President Roosevelt—the *late* President Roosevelt, more accurately. He'd died only a few weeks ago, and the whole country was still in mourning. This French radio program seemed to be playing snippets from Roosevelt's famous speeches. But this was something Grace hadn't heard before: a speech about the missing art in Europe.

"Whatever these paintings may have been to men who looked at them generations back—today they are not only works of art. Today they are the symbols of the human spirit, symbols of the world the freedom of the human spirit has made."

She shivered. *The freedom of the human spirit.*

Mr. Blythe hadn't known anything about the altarpiece's secrets, and had still been willing to risk his life to protect it. He'd known that art was worth fighting for.

It wasn't about hidden Clues or secret maps. Being a Cahill meant using your power to stop whatever evil was threatening the freedom of the human spirit.

Whatever the Vespers were looking for, they couldn't be allowed to find it. Someone had to save the altarpiece before it was too late.

She looked around the empty gallery.

And apparently, that someone was her.

Grace stared uneasily at the young woman next to her — a young woman who was piloting her in a battered, single-engine plane over the Austrian countryside. Being a Madrigal involved risks, but flying through German territory in a rickety plane was something else completely. It was a death wish.

Yet Jane Sperling — if that was even her real name — looked completely at ease as the tiny aircraft sputtered over eastern Switzerland.

Grace had a million questions for the mysterious girl. How did she know Rose? Why on earth would she be willing to take Grace to Austria? And what was her plan to keep them safe once they entered enemy airspace? Yet there was something about Jane's smirk that kept Grace from voicing any of her concerns.

"Sooo . . ." Grace tried one more time to extract a shred of information. "You're a friend of Rose's?"

Jane smiled but kept her eyes focused straight ahead. "That's right."

"You were in the Resistance with her?"

She laughed, which made her look much younger. She was closer to Grace's age than she'd realized. "If I were, do you think I would have lasted this long if I blabbed secrets to strangers?" Jane turned to look at Grace for the first time. "Rose said you speak German."

"Yes . . . *ja* . . . a little. But not enough to hide the fact that I'm American."

Jane turned back to the windshield. "That could be a problem." Grace stiffened, prompting a derisive snort from Jane. "If you are scared already, you are going to be in real trouble."

"If I weren't scared I'd be *insane*," Grace said, narrowing her eyes.

"And yet you're risking your life to find the Ghent altarpiece." She smiled. "You must be quite the art lover."

"It's a little bit more complicated than that," Grace snapped.

They flew on in silence. Jane fiddled with the controls on the instrument panel, and then sat up straighter. "We've crossed into Austria," she said.

The plane sank beneath the cloud cover, and the countryside came into view. It looked like something off a postcard—sparkling turquoise lakes were tucked among emerald green fields dotted with tiny houses with peaked roofs.

"Are you going back to France?" Grace asked.

Jane shook her head. "I have business to attend to in Bavaria." She turned to Grace. "That's in Germany."

"I *know*," Grace snapped.

A rumbling in the distance shook Grace's mind free of all thoughts except one. She gasped as a plane emerged from a bank of clouds, followed by two more. The wings each bore a black-and-white cross that she recognized from countless newsreels. Their tails bore large swastikas.

It was the Luftwaffe.

The German air force.

Without saying a word, Jane banked the plane sharply to the left, and Grace felt her stomach plummet to her toes. The German planes disappeared from view, but she could hear the buzz of their propellers close behind.

The green expanse of farmland was suddenly swept overhead as Jane took them into an inverted turn. Grace squeezed her eyes shut as the blood rushed to her head.

"Hang on!" Jane shouted as she leveled the plane and began picking up speed.

"Thank you for the warning!" Grace yelled, without opening her eyes. "I was just about to take a little nap."

Jane laughed as she pulled the throttle back as far as it would go. The plane began to shake.

"Open your eyes. You're missing the view."

The snowcapped peaks of the Austrian Alps glittered in the distance.

"Ch-ch-charming," Grace said, as the plane rattled violently. She clasped her hands over her stomach as a wave of nausea passed over her.

Grace yelped as the patter of gunfire pierced the roar of the engines. The plane rocked back and forth. She could hear the *ping* of bullets tearing into the wings.

Jane pushed the stick forward, sending the craft into a nosedive. They hurtled straight toward the ground. The farmhouses and trees below seemed to grow at an alarming speed. A scream burst out of Grace's chest but got lodged in her throat.

At the last minute, Jane straightened the plane and they glided over the tops of pine trees rustling in the wind. "Are you okay?"

Grace forced herself to swallow. "Never better."

Jane grinned as she turned in a large loop, skirting around the side of a steeply sloped mountain and entering a narrow valley. "We should be safe here. Those Luftwaffe planes are too large to maneuver through this pass."

The gap between the mountains was so small the sunlight filtered through the thick pine trees, giving it a greenish tinge. Emerald shadows filled the windows of the plane, making it seem like they'd flown through a portal to another realm. An enchanted world untouched by war. Unscathed by the Cahills.

But it seemed to have its own monsters.

Up ahead, a dark shape was hurtling toward them at an incomprehensible speed.

"Looks like I was wrong," Jane said, gritting her teeth. "There's a first time for everything."

In the past, dangerous situations had always made Grace feel more alive, giving her the energy to do whatever it took to survive. But now there was no escape. A strange numbness passed over her, as if her body was trying to get a head start on dying.

There was a rapid patter of gunfire as the approaching plane began shooting at them. Jane banked hard to the left until they were almost vertical, and then rotated one hundred eighty degrees in the opposite direction, swinging the plane back and forth like a pendulum.

The German plane was so close Grace could see the shape of the pilot through the windshield.

The only comforting thought was that, in less than ten seconds, he was going to be dead as well. Grace shut her eyes. She wanted to scream, but her throat wouldn't let any sound out.

Then she was weightless, floating through the air. *This must be what it feels like to die.*

Her stomach plummeted, as if it had parachuted out of the plane on its own. She opened her eyes and saw that they were suddenly flying low to the ground. The other plane was nowhere in sight.

"Woo-hoo!" Jane hollered. She reached over and slapped Grace on the shoulder. "I *knew* he'd fly over us at the last minute. Those Nazis are all cowards, when you get down to it."

They zoomed out of the valley and back into the sunlight, flying over a green meadow dotted with wildflowers.

"We're close to Altaussee. I am going to land here, and then you can hike down the mountain. Okay?"

"Absolutely," Grace said, regaining her breath. She pressed her nose to the window as she surveyed the area. There was no obvious military presence, but that didn't mean they weren't nearby. The Luftwaffe pilots had no doubt put the ground troops on high alert, and the German army would not take kindly to an American girl sneaking across their border. It wouldn't even be "shoot first, ask questions later." More like "shoot first, then throw the body in the lake."

There was a bump as the wheels hit the ground. After a very short taxi, Jane cut the engine, reached over Grace, and opened the door.

Grace unhooked her safety harness and turned to the pilot. "Thanks for the ride."

"Good luck. I hope to see you again someday, Grace."

Grace gave her a nod and jumped down. She watched as Jane restarted the engine, turned the plane around, and took off down the makeshift runway. Then she was gone, leaving Grace alone in one of the most dangerous countries on Earth.

When she reached the road, Grace turned left. Rose had told her the warehouse was somewhere in town, but the exact location was unknown. She might as well head downhill and try to get her bearings. Or at least think about how to avoid getting killed.

As she skidded down the steep, wildflower-lined path, Grace had to keep reminding herself that she was in enemy territory. It didn't matter that the houses all looked like they belonged in a cuckoo clock. The beautiful setting didn't change the fact that Austria was under control of one of the most ruthless military regimes in modern history.

The rumble of an approaching car sent her flying for cover, ducking behind a crumbling stone wall. As it turned a corner, Grace sat up and peeked over the edge. It was just a truck full of vegetables. She sighed. Her progress would be pretty slow going if she hid every time someone passed.

As she approached the town, the houses grew closer together. A small boy was playing with a dog in front of one of them. Grace took a deep breath and squared her shoulders. *Act like you belong*, she told herself. "*Guten Tag!*" she called cheerfully. The boy just stared at her. *Okay, so maybe Austrians aren't supposed to be friendly.* She just hoped she hadn't aroused too much suspicion.

A group of boys turned a corner and began walking toward her. One of them smiled at Grace, tipped his hat, and addressed her in rapid, heavily accented German. She felt her heart speed up. If she answered, they'd know she wasn't Austrian, and they might ask questions. Using her nerves to her advantage, she blushed and gave a shy smile. The boys laughed and continued on.

By the time Grace reached the village, her heart was thudding so loudly she was surprised the army hadn't been called in to investigate the commotion. Unsure what to do, she sat on a bench and tried her best to look Austrian. Whatever that meant.

The *clip-clop* of hooves caught her attention and she looked up. A bony gray horse was pulling a large wagon covered with a tarp. Although the driver looked like a normal farmer, Grace gasped when she saw the three men walking beside the wagon.

With their long coats, shiny tall boots, and red armbands, there was no mistaking them. They were members of the SS — the most elite — and deadly — unit in Hitler's army.

The SS had been one of the keys to Hitler's rise to power. They arrested people in the middle of the night. They tortured anyone they thought had useful information. Anyone who posed a threat was taken into a dark alley and shot. It didn't matter that Grace was only seventeen. That she was a girl. If she were caught, she'd be treated like a spy.

She'd be tortured.

Then killed.

"Alles in Ordnung, Fräulein?"

Grace looked up and found herself facing one of the officers. He had a curved scar that stretched from the corner of his mouth to the tip of his ear. His expression was inscrutable. He might have been commenting on the weather, or accusing her of treason.

"Ja," she croaked, praying he'd only said "How are you?"

The officer stared at her for a moment. Then he nodded, spun on his heel, and began marching back toward the wagon.

Grace half exhaled, half sobbed, burying her face in her sleeve. She had to get out of here. There was no way she was going to find the altarpiece. The only thing to do was try to escape with her life.

Grace looked up and saw the wagon turning a corner. The tarp didn't stretch all the way down, allowing her a glimpse of the cargo. It was dynamite.

It was true. They were going to blow up the altarpiece.

If she was correct about the dynamite, then chances were that wagon was heading to the secret storehouse. This was her best shot.

Grace leaped to her feet and scurried after the wagon. When the SS officers were looking the other way, she lifted the tarp and scrambled underneath it.

She was a mouse diving headfirst into a snake pit.

A mouse delusional enough to think it could save the world.

This is the stupidest thing I've ever done, Grace admitted to herself as she rocked back and forth with the movement of the wagon, struggling to keep her balance while sitting on a pile of fused dynamite.

After climbing steadily for about twenty minutes, the wagon stopped. The officers began barking orders in German, and she heard the clomp of approaching boots. Grace tunneled deeper under the mound of explosives, praying that they weren't planning on unloading it all at once. There was a flurry of shouting and activity, and Grace could feel the top layer of dynamite being carried off the wagon.

With every movement, the soldiers came closer to discovering her.

She didn't think her heart could race any faster, but then she felt a breeze brush against the back of her calf and realized her leg was exposed.

A strange numbness passed over her, as if the faster her heart beat, the slower the rest of her body became. In just a moment, it would stop forever. She was sure of it.

Would it hurt? Or would the soldiers just shoot her in the head and be done with it? She braced against the bottom of the wagon, waiting for the crack of the gun followed by . . . whatever came after.

"Halt!" a voice rang out. The movement in the wagon

stopped, and she heard the sound of footsteps growing fainter. Whoever had been unloading the wagon seemed to have moved away. Grace sat up slowly and crept to the edge. She took a breath and then peeked around the side.

To her surprise, she wasn't in the town. She'd assumed the art would be hidden in a fortified villa, or perhaps a discreet-looking warehouse. But the wagon had stopped halfway up a steep hill, next to the entrance of some sort of cave, or perhaps a mine. There were soldiers rushing in and out, giving orders to the workers carrying stacks of dynamite inside.

She ducked back behind the wagon as two long lines of soldiers marched by in rigid formation. The clomp of their boots could have been used as a metronome. They weren't wearing the elaborate uniforms of the SS officers, but they all had red armbands emblazoned with large black swastikas that made Grace's stomach churn with revulsion.

Something was definitely going on. Grace was no military expert, but she knew that you didn't send what looked like more than forty soldiers to guard a mine. Unless there was something important inside.

When the coast was clear, Grace darted from the wagon and dove behind a large rock next to the entrance. She caught her breath for a moment, and then peered around. Some of the dynamite was being loaded into metal trolleys whose tracks seemed to stretch down into the mine. If the altarpiece was some-where inside, the trolley would probably take her there.

She watched the movement of soldiers and work-ers for a moment, waiting for a break in the flow. Her heartbeat was loud but had slowed considerably, as if it were counting down the moments before she made the riskiest move of her life.

Three ... two ... go! Grace launched out from behind the rock, took a few flying steps, and leaped into the trolley, landing with a *clank* that shuddered through her whole body. She heard an officer bark another round of orders, and suddenly, the trolley began to move. She was heading into the mine.

The light faded rapidly as she rolled down the tracks. For a moment, she was swallowed by complete dark-ness, but then the trolley swept around a bend and Grace found herself in a passage lit with flickering bulbs. She listened for the sound of footsteps or voices, but there was nothing but the buzz of electricity.

Grace rose to her knees, wincing as she rubbed her elbows. Apparently, being a Madrigal meant spending your whole life black-and-blue. But as Grace looked up, her grimace collapsed into a gasp. This wasn't just a mine; it was a sophisticated storage facility. Metal shelves lined the stone walls, interspersed with heavy hooks.

But that wasn't what took Grace's breath away.

It was the paintings.

There were thousands of them hung in neat rows, stretching all the way down the passage until they disappeared into the darkness. Enormous oil paintings, smaller pastels, horizontal landscapes, and round portraits. She blinked, expecting the paintings to vanish, like the fragments of a dream fading in the sunlight. But there they were.

The trolley stopped and Grace climbed out. She glanced over her shoulder and dashed over to where a canvas tarp draped over a ladder. There were noises coming down the passageway, angry voices and stomping boots.

"What do you think you are doing?" a man whispered in English.

"Warum sprechen Sie auf Englisch?"

"I am speaking in English so that no one overhears me and panics," the first man answered. Grace peered through a hole in the tarp and saw a tall officer with silvery hair gritting his teeth with frustration. "The Allies are coming. They are less than ten miles away."

The other man, also wearing an officer's uniform, stared at him in shock. "What are our orders?"

The first man scowled. "We stuff the mine with dynamite, and light the fuse."

The second man glanced around, bewildered. "Without removing the art?"

"Ja," the first officer spat. "Now go fetch your men. *Schnell!*" He spun on his heel and marched away. The

second man muttered something in German and then followed.

Grace felt her knees buckle as she grasped on to the cold wall for balance. She probably had no more than five minutes to find the altarpiece. But then what? She didn't even have a gun. How was she supposed to keep it safe until the Allies arrived?

She glanced around to make sure the coast was clear and then stepped out from behind the ladder. A light in the next passageway caught her eye — a faint sparkle in the darkness. She walked toward it, feeling the air grow cooler as she moved deeper into the mine.

It was the angel Gabriel's wing, painted with exquisite gold leaf, glittering from an enormous painting.

It was the altarpiece.

She'd found it.

At first, she was simply mesmerized by the colors — vibrant hues she'd never even thought to imagine while looking at the black-and-white photos in her mother's book. It was uncanny to see the faces she knew so well displayed on such a grand scale — like seeing a movie star walking down the street. Some of them looked so realistic that Grace had trouble focusing her gaze. It almost felt rude to stare.

Grace looked around. The altarpiece was in a cave of sorts off the main passage into the mine. She rapped her knuckles against the stone wall. It felt strong enough to withstand at least a small explosion. But would that be enough to keep the "Lamb" safe if the Nazis lit the fuse?

If there were a way to seal off the entrance to the cave, the altarpiece might survive a larger blast. She dashed out into the passage. The trolley was still there, full of dynamite. She grabbed an armful of sticks and ran back to the altarpiece, silently cursing the faculty at Miss Harper's School for never teaching her anything useful.

Like explosives.

Ten minutes later, Grace stepped back to survey her handiwork. It was an admittedly shoddy job. Her Ekaterina cousin Bae Oh would certainly have laughed at her. But she'd wedged a stick of dynamite above the entrance to the cavern—far enough away to seal the entrance to the cave, but leave the walls, and the contents, intact.

If the explosion was too small, the guards would find her before she'd secured the "Lamb." They'd kill her and then destroy the altarpiece.

If the explosion was too big, it would destroy the whole mine—killing her and everyone in it. All those workers she'd seen filing in and out. They weren't Nazis—they were just men struggling to support their families in the only home they'd ever known.

Grace jumped as a shout rang through the mine. It was the officer. For all she knew, that could be his order for everyone to evacuate before they blew everything up.

There was no time to lose.

Grace pulled a matchbook out of her pocket and, with shaky fingers, extracted a match. She stared at it for a second before striking it against the stone wall. A tiny flame danced in the gloom. Grace took one last look at the altarpiece and whispered "Godspeed" before touching the match to the fuse.

For a moment, she felt like she was running in slow motion. Then there was a bone-shaking *boom* followed by a wave of heat. The force of the blast knocked Grace to the ground. She felt a jolt of pain in her wrist that was quickly overshadowed by a burning sensation in her foot.

She rolled onto her back, and saw that she was surrounded by thick black smoke.

Grace scrambled to her feet, shrieking as a flame scorched her calf and began traveling along the hem of her skirt. She beat it out with her hand, spun around, and began running for her life

She felt a wave of gravel and soot spray the back of her neck as she tore up the tracks. Halfway up, she found another empty trolley and dove inside, gasping for air as her body quaked from the effort. There was a chorus of shouts from above.

"*Sie sind hier!*" a voice screamed.

They're here.

"*Zerstör das Altarbild!*"

Destroy the altarpiece!

Grace heard some quiet mumbling, followed by a

screech that practically seared her eardrums.

"What do you mean, the cave is sealed?!"

She couldn't contain the laugh that bubbled out of her. Grace turned and saw a soldier standing over the trolley, his gun raised directly over her head. And then everything went dark.

"Miss . . . miss . . . Are you okay?" a voice called from somewhere far away.

She sat up and was overcome by a wave of nausea. The world was a sea of wavy blue and green lines that refused to come into focus. "Lie back down," the voice commanded as a large hand guided her head back to the ground. She blinked and saw someone standing over her. He was tall, and wearing a very dirty uniform.

"Who are you?" Grace croaked. Her mouth felt like it was full of ash.

"You're *American*?" He lowered himself down to the ground and stared at her. "I'm Lieutenant Greene. What in God's name are you doing in Austria?"

"Is the altarpiece okay?" she asked, trying to sit up. The Allies had obviously arrived, but what had happened to the "Lamb"?

"How do you know about that?" he asked, his eyes widening. "Who are you?"

Grace ignored the question. "I . . . I . . . " She inhaled sharply. "I think I might've blown it up." Just saying the words was enough to start her body shaking.

"Whoa! Calm down there." Lieutenant Greene grabbed her shoulders. "It's fine. We have a map of the storage facility — or whatever this thing is. The altarpiece was in its own cave that was somehow sealed off. It's under some rubble, but our engineers think that it's most likely intact."

Grace sighed, lowered herself back to the ground, and closed her eyes.

"Just stay there," she heard Lieutenant Greene say. "The medics are on their way. Don't worry, we'll get you back home safe."

Safe.

The altarpiece hadn't been destroyed. The Cahills still had a chance to learn what the Vespers were after and figure out a way to stop them.

Someday, the word *safe* would mean something again.

She took a deep breath, inhaling the scent of pine that punctuated the smoky air, and smiled. If you had to be lying half-unconscious somewhere, the Austrian Alps weren't the worst place to be.

She had a feeling she was going to end up in much stranger places before this thing was over. She wasn't going to hide from it any longer — the Clues or the fight against the Vespers.

The Vespers had been right to send Mlle Hubert after her. Grace *was* a threat.

And she was just getting started.

PART 3

London, 2008

Ian Kabra took a sip of espresso and grimaced.

A flash of annoyance crossed the young woman's face. "Is it all right, *sir?*" she asked, raising an over-plucked eyebrow. She was probably an art student who thought interning at an auction house meant cataloging Monets, not serving drinks to fourteen-year-olds.

The espresso was perfectly revolting, but the auction was about to begin, and Ian needed to focus on bidding strategy. Besides, just looking at the girl's acrylic blend cardigan made his skin itch. Why anyone would wear anything other than cashmere was beyond him. "It's fine, thank you."

She smirked. "Are you sure you wouldn't rather a hot chocolate?"

"I am quite accustomed to drinking coffee . . . Fiona," Ian said, glancing at the girl's name tag. "Only *this* tastes like it was brewed with the liquid that collects at the bottom of my horse's trough." Ian gave her the smile he normally reserved for attractive people—or very, very rich homely ones. "It'll have to do, though. Now run along and go back to texting your no-doubt captivating friends, or whatever you thought was more important than making a proper espresso."

Fiona opened her mouth to reply, but shut it quickly as an elegant older woman came gliding toward them. She clasped Ian's hand warmly. "Lovely to see you, Mr. Kabra. I trust your parents are well?"

"Quite well, thank you, Mrs. Hatfield. Mummy sends her regards. She was unfortunately held up in Paris."

"Oh, dear. How inconvenient," she said mildly. Ian knew Mrs. Hatfield was imagining his mother trying on scarves at an expensive boutique, or perhaps sipping champagne in an exclusive restaurant. But Ian's parents weren't just fabulously wealthy art dealers—they were the heads of the most elite branch of the Cahill family, the Lucians, and they were currently spearheading a plan to find the remaining 39 Clues—the key to the family's historic power. The other branches tended to call the Lucians' talent for blackmail, sabotage, and the odd assasination "ruthless," but that was just because they didn't have what it took to win.

Ian smiled. "She sent me to have a look at your Van Eyck."

"Ah, yes of course," Mrs. Hatfield said rather breathlessly. "It is a very special piece. Although"—she glanced around the room, which was filling with men in dark suits and women in black dresses and high heels — "I have a feeling the bidding is going to be rather *lively.*" She placed her hand on Ian's shoulder. "I hope your mother won't be too disappointed if you don't manage to win it for her, dear. This sort of thing takes some practice, you know."

Ian broadened his smile as he shrugged her hand away. "We'll just have to wait and see."

The first portion of the auction was horrendously dull. Ian flipped through the latest issue of *Horse & Hound* while a few middle-aged ladies squabbled over paintings of fruit and chubby angels.

"And that's lot number fourteen, 'Still Life with Poppies,' sold for four hundred, seventy-five thousand pounds." The auctioneer banged his gavel on the podium. "Next, we have lot number fifteen, 'Self-Portrait of the Artist' by Jan Van Eyck." A murmur rippled through the audience as the display case rotated to reveal the painting. Works by the fifteenth-century Flemish master rarely came up for sale, and this piece would be the crowning jewel of any collection.

Ian didn't particularly care for the painting of the scowling old man who looked like he could benefit from teeth whitening. But he knew that if his mother wanted it, it probably had an important connection to the Clue hunt.

"The bidding will start at" — the auctioneer looked down at his notes — "two million pounds."

The woman next to Ian whistled. "Not exactly

chump change, is it?" she said in an American accent. "What is that? About a million bucks?"

Ian gave her a tight smile. "Try four million."

"Do I have two million?" the auctioneer drawled. A man in the second row raised his numbered paddle. The auctioneer nodded. "That's two million. Do I have two point five?" A woman standing off to the side raised hers.

Ian leaned back in his chair and stretched his long legs forward. There was no reason to waste his energy waving his hand in the air like some trained monkey. The first bidder didn't have a chance of winning the painting. While his suit appeared to be high quality, Ian could see the man's car keys poking out of his pocket. If he had to drive himself to the auction, he'd never be able to afford a Van Eyck.

He turned his attention to the woman, who after raising her bid to four million, leaned in to whisper to her companion. Her face had gone quite red. She would chicken out before long.

Ian scanned the crowd, looking for the *real* players. A red-haired woman holding a Pomeranian looked promising. And the young man speaking discreetly into his mobile was surely receiving instructions from an absentee bidder. Ian removed his own mobile from his pocket and raised it up as if he were looking for a signal. The phone was custom designed for Lucian agents and contained a hacking application. He activated the program, and a few seconds later, a text transcription of the young man's conversation began scrolling across the screen. He was authorized to go up to ten million pounds. Brilliant.

"That's six million pounds to the gentleman in the front. Do I have seven?"

Ian's mobile buzzed. He had a new text from his mother.

WE'LL PICK YOU UP IN FIVE

It was time to hurry things along. He used his mobile to access the banking information of his most promising competitors. Their most recent transfers would give him an idea of how much they were willing to spend.

"Seven million to the gentleman in the back. Do I have eight?"

Ian made some quick calculations in his head, then raised his own paddle. "Sixteen point four million pounds," he called out breezily.

A silence fell over the room. The auctioneer blinked a few times. "Come again, sir?"

"Sixteen point four million," Ian said, rising to his feet. "Now, can we move it along? I haven't got all day."

The auctioneer cleared his throat. "That's sixteen point four million pounds going once . . ." Ian saw a few people shift uncomfortably in their seats, as if reconsidering their decisions. "Going twice . . ." The red-haired woman started to lift her paddle, but then lowered it quickly. "Sold to the young gentleman in the back."

Ian strode to the front of the room, ignoring the murmurs bubbling up from the crowd like clumsily poured champagne. The auctioneer smiled. "If you'll kindly follow Mrs. Hatfield, she'll arrange for delivery," he said as two uniformed guards carefully removed the painting from the display.

"I'll take it with me now, actually."

The auctioneer's brow furrowed with confusion. "Are you going to put it in your *car*?"

His phone buzzed again.

WE'RE OUTSIDE

Ian spun on his heel, and beckoned for the guards to follow him with the painting. He made his way into the chandelier-lit hallway and down the marble stairs. When he reached the entrance to the auction house, the doorman held up his hand. "Just a moment, please, sir. There's some sort of commotion outside."

But Ian pushed right past him and stepped into the street. Leaves and bits of paper swirled through the air as if a tornado had swept through London. Pedestrians were crouched behind mailboxes, or stood huddled in doorways.

"Please, Mr. Kabra, wait!" Ian turned and saw the auctioneer standing beside him, gasping for breath. "You can't treat a Van Eyck like a bag of takeaway fish and chips!"

A shadow descended over the street and the wind

picked up even more. There were a few faint screams as a sleek black helicopter came into view and lowered to the ground.

Mummy had arrived.

"That can't be legal," one of the awestruck guards muttered over the roar of the rotors.

Ian rolled his eyes. Laws were for poor people.

That's why it was good to be a Kabra.

Isabel Kabra smiled as Ian carefully placed the painting on the leather seat, and then sat down next to it. "Well done, darling," she said, giving the portrait an appraising look.

The helicopter rose into the air. Out the window, he could see pedestrians scattering like flustered pigeons. His eleven-year-old sister, Natalie, scowled from her seat next to their mother. "I think it's horrid. I won't have it in *my* room."

"We'll make room for it in the gallery," Isabel said, fishing through her purse for her ringing BlackBerry. "Hello?" She held her free hand out in front of her to examine her French manicure. It was flawless, as usual. "Yes, this is she. . . . Ian wasn't in history class this afternoon?" She placed her hand over her mouth in an expression of mock horror, and then grinned at Ian. "Of course he wasn't. He's ill, the poor dear. . . . I completely forgot to ring you, I'm dreadfully sorry. . . . Yes, I'll make sure he gets his assignments. . . . I quite agree, the French Revolution *is* very important. . . . Thank you, Ms. Wilcox. Good-bye." Isabel smiled as she placed her phone in her lap. "As if that spinster could possibly teach *you* anything about the French Revolution."

Natalie shuddered and brought her hands to her neck. Marie Antoinette and her husband, King Louis XVI, had been Lucians, of course. But they'd unfortunately lost their heads because some uppity peasants had decided they were bored of being poor.

"Stop being so dramatic." Ian rolled his eyes. "That wouldn't happen today." The Lucian branch controlled the governments of nearly every superpower on earth. His mother could mobilize an army faster than most mums could make one of those vile things poor people liked to eat. Sandwiches.

"Quite right, darling," Isabel said as she scrolled through her e-mails. Her face lit up and she read something on the screen. "That's marvelous," she muttered.

"What's marvelous, Mummy?" Natalie asked, leaning over to look at Isabel's phone.

Isabel slipped the BlackBerry back in her purse. "It looks like Ian won't have the great pleasure of listening to the next installment of Ms. Wilcox's French Revolution lecture after all."

Natalie clasped her hands together. "Are we going on holiday?" she squealed.

A mischievous smile played across Isabel's lips, and Ian felt a flutter in his stomach.

"Are we going on a *mission*?" he asked, working hard to maintain the slightly bored tone he'd learned from his parents. He and Natalie had been training for the Clue hunt their whole lives. When most children went to football practice or ballet class, Ian and Natalie were studying cryptography, or learning how to skydive. Yet while they'd accompanied their father, Vikram, on a midnight "visit" to the British Museum, and distracted the Chinese ambassador while Isabel copied his hard drive, neither Ian nor Natalie had ever been sent on a solo Clue-hunting trip.

Natalie didn't even try to contain her excitement. She knelt on the seat and leaned toward Isabel. "Tell us, Mummy," she said, bouncing up and down slightly, oblivious to the wrinkles she was creating in her pink dress. Although an eleven-year-old girl who favored ruffled frocks wasn't the most obvious choice for a secret agent, Ian knew his sister would be up to the task. She had deadly aim and could take down any target with either a tranquilizer gun or a cutting remark about their outfit.

However, it was important that she knew who was in charge. "Calm down, Natalie," he said, making a show of leaning back in his seat. "You look like one of Granny's terriers begging for a treat."

Natalie narrowed her eyes. "Don't pretend like you don't care." She smirked. "You've probably already decided what to pack in Mr. Buttons's traveling trunk."

Ian opened his mouth to reply, but then saw his mother raising her eyebrow. According to Isabel, it was unbecoming to bicker like peasant children.

"We're leaving for Belgium early tomorrow morning," Isabel said. "An Ekaterina at the University of Ghent is developing a tool for art restoration that your father and I believe will be quite useful." She paused and then smiled. "You two are going to fetch us the plans from his computer so our engineers can build a model."

Natalie squealed, and Ian felt his stomach twist in a way that had nothing to do with the helicopter's sudden descent. After years of preparation, and countless hours of training, he was finally going on a real mission. "Are you going to brief us this evening?" Ian asked.

The helicopter banked to the left, and the vast green lawn of the Kabra estate slid into view. "Irina's waiting for you in the library. She'll explain everything." Ian saw Natalie scrunch up her face. Neither of them cared for Irina Spasky, the high-ranking Russian agent who was sent on all the most important missions. Irina might think he and Natalie were being given special treatment because of their parents, but they'd prove her wrong.

Ian wasn't just the son of Vikram and Isabel Kabra. He was a Lucian, through and through.

It was time to show the world what he could do.

As they made their way from the landing pad up to the house, Ian saw a gardener duck behind the thick hedge. Isabel was strict about the staff keeping out of sight, especially on the grounds. She said nothing ruined a lovely view like a wheelbarrow being pushed by an unattractive man in coveralls.

And it was a lovely view. Ian had seen enough of the world to know that the Kabras' London residence was truly extraordinary. The mansion had been built in the eighteenth century for the Duke of Hampshire and, from the outside, there was nothing to suggest that that the present owners had spent millions of pounds transforming it into a state-of-the-art command center—the center of operations for the most powerful group of people on the planet.

The door swung open, revealing their butler, Bickerduff. "Good afternoon, madam," he said in the hushed, reverent tone that always reminded Ian of a funeral director. "Would you care for some tea?"

"Not now. Did the Chanel people deliver my gown for the benefit?"

"Yes, madam."

"And did the documents from the prime minister arrive?"

"I took the liberty of placing them on your desk, madam."

"Thank you, Bickerduff." She turned to Ian and

Natalie. "Now run along, darlings. Irina is waiting."

Ian handed his jacket to Bickerduff and then strode toward the massive marble staircase that divided the east and west wings of the house. Natalie scampered after him. "What do you think they want the tool for?" she asked, bounding up the steps two at a time in order to keep pace with Ian.

"I don't know," he said, doing his best to sound like his whole body wasn't buzzing with nerves and excitement. But he couldn't keep himself from speeding up as they passed the landing. Natalie darted ahead, swerving to avoid the enormous urn Isabel had found during a mission to Greece.

Natalie waited for him at the top of the stairs. She probably didn't want to go into the library alone. They turned down a long hallway lined with portraits of famous Lucians throughout the centuries. During the day, Ian barely noticed the paintings. But at night, the light from the flickering lamps cast strange shadows on the wall and created the illusion that the figures' eyes were following him.

Halfway down the hall, a door opened and Ian's father emerged from his study, followed by a man he'd never seen before. Vikram was smiling, but the stranger appeared somewhat ill, and his wrinkled, sweat-stained shirt looked particularly grubby compared to Vikram's perfectly pressed gray suit, complete with a red silk pocket square.

"Ah, and here they come now," Vikram said as

he caught sight of them. "The most expensive stocks in my portfolio. Andrew, this is my son, Ian, and my daughter, Natalie. Children, Mr. Pringle."

Ian reached out to shake the man's hand, but all Mr. Pringle did was flinch.

"I heard you did splendidly today," Vikram continued, ignoring his guest's strange behavior. He turned to Mr. Pringle. "Ian just picked up a rather marvelous Van Eyck at auction. Shall we go have a look before dinner? I'd quite like to hear your expert opinion." Mr. Pringle paled slightly but followed wordlessly.

As their footsteps faded away, Ian and Natalie continued down the hallway and stepped into the library. The late-afternoon light streaming through the tall windows made the room look almost cheerful despite the rows of animal heads mounted along the far wall. Ian glanced over at Natalie and saw that her eyes were pointed toward the maroon carpet. Although she'd never admit it, she hated having to look at the dead animals.

Ian wrinkled his nose. The unpleasant but familiar smell of old books was punctuated by another scent—industrial strength hair spray.

Irina was sitting on the leather couch, restlessly tapping her fingers on an antique globe. Her long red nails were boring into Iceland and Norway like heat-guided missiles.

"Stop that," Ian said, walking toward her. "You'll ruin it."

Irina's glare intensified. "Your parents have already ruined *you*." She seemed to take it as a personal offense that he and Natalie hadn't grown up standing in bread lines, shivering in the bleak Soviet snow. "Such disrespectful children, I have never seen."

Ian rolled his eyes at Natalie. "Yes, well, so sorry to disappoint. Now what is it you're supposed to show us?"

Irina sighed. "I still do not understand why Vikram and Isabel place future of Lucian branch in hands of children." She sneered, revealing slightly discolored teeth. "Hands that do not know the meaning of work." She got up from the couch and walked over to the long glass-top table at the end of the library. Ian and Natalie exchanged glances and then followed her.

The table was covered with photos of a tall, modern-looking building and floor plans of what Ian assumed to be the inside. "Is that the university?" Ian asked.

"Some spy," Irina scoffed. "Perhaps you can post photo to Internet and ask your Bookface friends to confirm."

Before Ian had a chance to respond, Natalie piped in. "And perhaps *you* can stop wasting time and do your duty." She raised her small chin. "I believe you're meant to brief us on the mission. You may proceed."

Irina stared at Natalie for a moment, her face unreadable. Then she plunged the nail of her index finger into one of the photos. "This is physics lab at University of Ghent." She turned to Ian. "That is in Belgium."

He gritted his teeth. "I know."

"Your mother believes one of the professors is Ekaterina and that his research has something to do with a Clue. She wants you two to break into lab, hack into computer, and copy his files."

He slid into one the chairs surrounding the table and motioned for Natalie to do the same. "So what do you have in mind?" Ian asked lazily, as if Irina were merely a shop assistant eager to sell him some new shoes.

Irina stared at him, her eye twitching slightly. Another one of the agent's irresistible charms. Then she pointed to one of the photos and began a rapid overview of the mission. Ian and Natalie were going to break in through the service entrance at dawn — there was a ten-minute window of time when the alarm system reset. Then they'd have to sneak up to the professor's lab. "Here is entry code," Irina said, passing Ian a slip of paper. "Memorize and destroy it."

"If it's an Ekaterina stronghold, how did we get the code?" Natalie asked.

Irina's eye twitched as she turned away from them. "Your mother has her methods."

Something about her tone made Ian uneasy, but he pushed the thought aside. "Very well, then. Everything seems to be in order," he said.

Any rogue feelings of nervousness he might have had were swept away by excitement. By the time Ms. Wilcox began droning on about the French

Revolution, he'd have completed his first real Lucian mission. He could already imagine the look on Isabel's face when he and Natalie presented her with the Ekat files.

Some children drew pictures for their parents. Ian and Natalie stole top secret information that would help them take over the world.

He turned to his sister and grinned.

This was going to be fun.

There were still a few minutes left before dinner, so when Natalie ran off to IM her friends, Ian wandered into the control room next to his mother's office. When he was younger, he used to spend hours in front of the wall of monitors watching live feeds from Cahill hot spots around the world. Some of the screens showed bustling activity, like the swarms of tourists buzzing around the base of the Eiffel Tower or at the entrance to Neuschwanstein Castle. Others looked more like screen savers; no matter how long he stared at the Bermuda Triangle monitor, all he ever saw was an endless procession of gray-blue waves. Yet they all filled him with the same giddy anticipation—these were all places he'd be sent to explore one day. It was like watching a film trailer for the rest of his life.

Ian glanced quickly over his shoulder and walked over to the far side of the wall, crouching down to look at the screen in the bottom corner. There was rarely any interesting activity on this monitor but — he looked down at his watch — it was almost the end of the school day in Boston. He stared at the image of the dull apartment building flanked by scraggly trees, waiting for something to happen but not allowing himself to admit what he was waiting for.

Just as he was about to turn around, a flash of color caught his eye. Amy Cahill was walking up the front path, her long auburn hair blowing wildly in the autumn wind. Her cheap green parka looked like it had come straight out of the discount pile. He leaned in for a better look. The color *did* bring out the reddish tones in her hair, but he was sure that was just a lucky coincidence. Whenever he saw Amy at one of her grandmother's dreadful Cahill gatherings, she redefined the term *walking disaster*.

Poor people were such an enigma. He knew that not everyone could afford to fly to Paris to get their hair cut, but surely there was someone in the state of Massachusetts who could keep Amy Cahill from looking like an Irish setter left out in the rain.

Or not, Ian thought, cringing as he watched Amy flick a damp leaf off the hem of her horrid jeans. What was it about Americans that made them so uncouth?

The dinner bell rang. Ian stood up and stretched. When the Lucians found the 39 Clues and unlocked whatever legendary power they were meant to provide,

Ian's first order of business would be reclaiming the American colonies. It was for their own good, really.

He turned to the screen for one last look at Amy Cahill, but she had disappeared inside the building.

By the time Ian made it down to the dining room, everyone else was already seated. Vikram and Isabel were in their usual spots at the ends of the long table, and Natalie was sitting across from their visitor. Ian sat next to his sister and placed the stiff cloth napkin in his lap. He was used to having guests at dinner, but they were normally foreign dignitaries, or local billionaires — people who generally didn't have sweat stains blossoming on their rumpled shirts. Mr. Pringle looked even more anxious than he had upstairs. It was clear he was unaccustomed to dining in such a setting, and was probably nervous about using the wrong fork or making some other plebeian error. It was like watching a mouse that had just been dropped into a snake tank — his eyes were wide and he kept glancing over his shoulder, as if frantically trying to find a hidden escape route.

A line of servers emerged from the concealed doorway with the first course, foie gras with caviar. "I'm delighted you could join us, Mr. Pringle," Isabel called from the end of the table, her melodic voice echoing through the vast dining room. "You're a difficult man to track down."

Mr. Pringle's fork clattered to the floor. "I've been t-t-traveling. For my research."

"Yes. I understand you're publishing a book on Northern Renaissance art. I just adore Flemish painting." She took a dainty bite of foie gras before continuing. "So full of hidden meaning, wouldn't you agree?"

He gulped. "I suppose."

"I've always been particularly intrigued by the Ghent altarpiece. Such a fascinating history. Is it true it's been the subject of more theft attempts than any other work of art in the world?"

"Yes," Mr. Pringle said, a measure of assurance strengthening his voice. Awkward people always bucked up when discussing their little hobbies. Even Amy Cahill's dreadful stammer disappeared when you let her prattle on about books. "Seven times, actually."

"Now, why is that?" Vikram asked.

"Oh, it varied," Mr. Pringle said, picking up his butter knife. "Religious reasons. Political reasons. One of the panels was stolen just before the Second World War and was never found."

"That's right," Isabel responded sweetly. "It was replaced with a reproduction, wasn't it? It makes one wonder if perhaps the rumors are true."

"Rumors?" Mr. Pringle asked. The hand holding the knife began to tremble, preventing him from making contact with his dinner roll.

"You know," Isabel said, patting her mouth with her napkin, although there wasn't a trace of anything on her face. "About the map."

Mr. Pringle's knife clattered to the floor. "It's a myth. There's no evidence to suggest that the altarpiece contains a map of any sort." He waved his empty hand over his roll, apparently forgetting that he was no longer holding a knife. Bickerduff materialized beside him and handed Mr. Pringle a new one. "Th-th-thank you," Mr. Pringle said, looking over his shoulder. But Bickerduff had already slipped away.

"It's a shame your wife couldn't join us," Isabel said as she cut a small sliver of meat. "I understand she's an art historian as well. Does she share your opinions about the altarpiece? I'd love to hear her thoughts on the rumors."

Mr. Pringle raised his head and looked at Isabel directly for the first time. "She's on holiday," he said with surprising firmness. "She'll be out of the country for some time. It would be pointless to try to contact her."

Out of the corner of his eye, Ian thought he saw his father stiffen, but Isabel smiled. "Oh, I don't know about that. It's remarkable what you can do with the right resources." She lifted a crystal decanter in the air. "More wine?"

Mr. Pringle took a deep breath, but then pressed his lips together and waited a moment before replying. "She doesn't have the information you want. Neither of us does."

Ian wondered why his mother was wasting her time quizzing this blundering fool. He was obviously useless.

Isabel placed the decanter back on the table and then turned to Ian and Natalie. "Time for bed, children."

"But we haven't even had pudding," Natalie said, crossing her arms.

"You have a big day tomorrow, darling. Off you toddle."

Natalie grunted and then stomped out noisily. As Ian rose to follow her, Mr. Pringle shifted in his seat. "I should probably be going as well."

"Oh, you can't." Isabel's eyes widened. "Not before dessert. Our pastry chef is an absolute genius."

"You're too kind, but it's getting rather late. . . ." He trailed off.

Vikram's chair scraped against the marble floor as he stood up. "Of course. There's just the small matter of that . . . transaction. If you follow me, we can finish our discussion in the East wing."

Ian paused. The East wing was the command center. No one but high-ranking agents was allowed anywhere near the entrance, and he was certain that this quivering wreck was not a Cahill, let alone a Lucian.

Mr. Pringle forced his mouth into a pathetic semblance of a grin. "B-but your library is so charming. Can't we speak there?"

Isabel rose and glided toward their guest. He scrambled to his feet so quickly he almost knocked over his chair. "Oh, I think you'll be more comfortable in the study. Once my husband starts talking about the Ghent altarpiece, it can be hard to get him to stop. Do come this way." She placed her hand on Mr. Pringle's elbow and guided him past Ian out of the room.

Ian was too excited to sleep. It didn't matter that the thick velvet curtains blocked out all light, shrouding his bedroom in complete darkness. It didn't matter that he'd already rung Bickerduff for hot cocoa twice. He couldn't stop going over the plans for the next day. He'd swallowed the information so quickly he could almost feel it bouncing around in his stomach. They were supposed to try to hack the key reader on the side entrance. If that didn't work, they'd have to scale the side of the building and crawl through the air vents on the roof.

Had Bickerduff packed his climbing shoes? Ian sat up and was about to ring the bell a third time when a sound rose up from the bottom of the house. Almost like a man's scream. A terrifying notion scurried across his brain before darting into a hidden den of dark thoughts. *They're probably watching a film*, Ian told himself, trying to ignore the fact that he'd never seen his parents use the DVD player.

A stream of bright light pierced the darkness of the room. He sat up and squinted, shielding his eyes from the glare. "Natalie?" he whispered as the blurry figure came into focus. "What are you doing?"

She crept in and closed the door. "Have you seen my Gucci sunglasses?"

"What?" He rubbed his eyes. "What are you talking about?"

Natalie took a few steps forward and then leaped onto his bed like a small pajama-wearing dog. "I can't find my sunglasses. What if I need them in Belgium?"

Ian glanced over at the clock on his night table. "It's half twelve, Nat. Can you look for them in the morning?"

Another one of the strange sounds clawed at the silence of the house. This time, it sounded more like a shriek than a shout. Ian saw Natalie's eyes widen in the faint light and suddenly understood the real reason for her midnight visit.

"They must be watching television." It sounded even less convincing when he said it aloud. Natalie didn't answer, and instead curled up on the foot of his bed.

Ian wasn't sure how much time passed before the noises stopped. But he still couldn't fall asleep.

The silence was even worse than the screams.

A few hours later, they were airborne again, this time in the private jet instead of the helicopter. It was still dark—Isabel had sent Bickerduff to wake them up at three A.M.—and the lights of London glinted dimly in early morning mist.

Natalie was next to him, fast asleep. But Ian could barely manage to close his eyes. He sank back in his leather seat, staring at the untouched croissant in front of him. As the plane juddered through some turbulence, the china plate rattled on the plastic tray. He knew he should try to eat something, but his stomach was writhing like a frantic caged animal—he could almost feel it trying to climb out of his throat.

He looked over at his mother, who was perched on a seat across the aisle, calmly typing on her BlackBerry.

Despite the ungodly hour, Isabel's gray shift dress was perfectly pressed and her hair was up in a smooth twist. He'd actually never seen his mother in a nightgown or robe. Running the world's most powerful secret organization didn't allow for much downtime. But it was worth it. The Kabras didn't need to lounge around in bed, watching *Ping-Pong with the Stars*. That was one of the many things that set them apart. It wasn't just their enormous wealth, their impeccable breeding, or astonishing good looks. When they wanted something, they didn't rest until they got it.

Isabel glanced up from her phone and caught his eye. "All right there, sweetheart? Do you not like the croissant?" She smiled. "We can't have you go off on your first mission on an empty stomach."

"I'm not very hungry."

"Don't be nervous, darling. You and Natalie are

going to do splendidly. All your hard work is going to pay off. You're going to waltz into that building, fetch me the files, and walk back out in five minutes flat. My only concern is that you'll find it too easy." She reached over and squeezed his knee. "We'll come up with something a bit more fun for you next time. It's about time we started taking advantage of your talents."

The wild creature in Ian's stomach stopped thrashing and curled into a contented little ball, sending a flood of warmth throughout his body. He felt his mouth stretch into a wide grin that would look ridiculous on camera, but what did he care? He was off to perform his first real mission as a Lucian agent.

Suddenly, his eyelids felt heavy and he leaned back, allowing his body to sink into the soft leather.

Before his eyes closed completely, he took one last glance at his mother. She had returned to her phone and looked just as alert as before. Perhaps she never slept at all. He heard that sharks never went to sleep. They never stopped swimming. Never stopped hunting.

Ian knew he'd be like that someday. But for now, he needed to rest.

There was a sleek black sedan waiting for them at the private airfield outside of Ghent. It was almost dawn, and the car zipped through the silent city as if trying to outrace the sun rays that had begun to shine out over the tops of the peaked roofs.

While London was a mix of old and new, the buildings in Ghent had been remarkably well preserved. With its narrow streets flanked by pointy Gothic and sprawling Renaissance buildings, the city seemed like something out of a fairy tale, making the modern cars parked alongside the road look like they'd been spat out of a time machine gone haywire.

By now, both he and Natalie were wide awake, sitting up on either side of Isabel. The car turned onto a larger boulevard and sped away from the historic city center, toward the university. The closer they got, the faster Ian's heart began to beat. He leaned away from his mother, worried that she'd be able to feel it.

"All right," Isabel said cheerfully as a cluster of modern high-rises appeared in the distance. "I'm going to drop you two off by the side entrance. Then Hendrik will drive the car around the block to avoid suspicion. You have ten minutes before the morning cleaning staff arrives. Did you synchronize your watches?" Ian and Natalie both nodded. "Wonderful." She beamed. "Your father and I are so lucky to have such clever children." She reached over and grabbed each of their hands. "Now make sure to stay together, no matter what."

The car slowed to a stop. There was a faint *click* as Hendrik unlocked the doors. The ordinary sound had never felt so ominous. Isabel leaned over and gave each of them a kiss on the cheek. "Off you go, duckies. I know you'll make me proud."

Ian opened the door and slid out into the cool morning air, stepping to the side to make room for Natalie. The physics building was twenty-two stories of glass and metal that shimmered under the rising sun. Despite its large, light-filled windows, it struck Ian as impenetrable as a fort. His palms grew sweaty as he craned his neck to see the roof. The backup plan—climbing to the top to enter through the air vents—suddenly seemed insane. Ian readjusted the backpack that held his rappelling gear and other tools, silently praying that he wouldn't have to use it.

"There's an extraction helicopter on standby, right?" Ian asked. It was standard Lucian practice to have one at the ready during missions, in case of emergencies.

"Isn't there always?" Isabel said quickly, glancing down at her phone. "Oh, and one more thing. Make sure you reactivate the alarm when you leave. It's the same code." She slid over and grabbed the door handle. "Good luck, darlings."

"Bye, Mummy," Natalie called as Isabel shut the door. The car drove away and turned a corner. She was gone.

Ian nodded at Natalie, and they jogged down a gravel path, which led to an alley along the side of the building. Without saying a word, they pressed themselves against the wall and glanced around, but the coast was clear.

There was an electronic key reader next to the door. Natalie reached into her backpack and pulled out a plastic card. She waved it across the sensor, which produced a series of beeps. She pressed a few numbers on the keypad, and the door swung open. Ian exhaled loudly. He hadn't even realized he'd been holding his breath.

With one more glance behind them, he and Natalie stepped into the basement of the building. It was unlikely that the university had installed motion sensors in what appeared to be a janitorial supply room but, just to be safe, he pressed his back against the wall and inched toward the door at the other end. He peered around the corner, and then signaled for Natalie to follow him into the hallway.

They moved quickly but silently down the dark corridor and up the emergency staircase to the fourth floor, where the Ekaterina professor had his lab. The sun had risen high enough to flood the hallway with faint light and illuminate the colorful posters on the wall. There were huge satellite photos of the planets interspersed with flyers advertising student events. Or, at least, that's what Ian assumed. It was hard to tell when everything was written in Dutch.

Despite his nervousness, Ian grinned. It was amusing to think of the university students all over the world, taking classes, making plans for the future, when really, it was Ian's family who made all the decisions. Being a Cahill was all that really mattered. And

Ian and Natalie were about to establish themselves as two of its rising stars.

"Ian," Natalie hissed. "What are you doing?"

He'd stopped without realizing it. His cheeks flushed as he jogged to catch up with Natalie, who was waiting for him in front of a set of heavy double doors. Lab number 403. This was it. Unlike the other rooms along the hall, this one had warning signs affixed to the small plastic windows. INGANG VERBODEN.

There was a keypad on the wall. Ian raised his hand and saw that it was shaking. *Calm down*, he scolded himself. *Everything is going according to plan.* He turned to Natalie. "Four-eight-one-eight, right?" She nodded.

Ian entered the code and held his breath. There was an agonizing moment of silence followed by a reassuring low beep. It worked. "Ready?" He reached forward, pushed on the bar, and opened the door.

The large, windowless room was dark. Long lab tables were arranged in neat rows, and the shelves were full of equipment. Ian recognized the beakers and microscopes from science class, but most of the tools were unfamiliar.

There was a computer on each table, but the desk at the front of the room had the largest, newest-looking monitor. That had to be it. Ian motioned for Natalie to follow him as he darted over to the desk and tapped the keyboard. They both jumped as it pinged to life, and then got to work.

Natalie inserted a flash drive into the USB port while Ian performed a search for the files. According to Irina, Professor Hauser's project had the code name Archimedes. An error message popped up. *Password required.* He took a deep breath and flexed his fingers, then began furiously typing as he opened the program he'd learned from his hacking tutor. The screen turned black for a moment, then lines of code began scrolling across. Ian clicked on the folder again. It opened, showing six documents labeled *Archimedes*.

"We did it!" Natalie whispered.

"*I* did it," Ian said, smiling as he copied the folder onto the USB drive. "Now come on. Let's get out of here." He placed the drive in his pocket, turned off the monitor, and headed toward the door.

They walked back and Ian turned to the keypad and typed in the same code they'd used to enter: 4-8-1-8. A message flashed across the screen.

INDRINGER

Before Ian had time to react, a high-pitched alarm rang out from somewhere down the hallway. Natalie gasped and Ian whirled around. Red lights had begun flashing and a stream of beeps joined in with the alarm.

Don't panic, he thought, forcing himself to breathe. They were in a university physics lab, for goodness' sake, not the Pentagon. At worst, some part-time security guard would come lumbering down the hall, and Ian and Natalie would just pretend to be lost. He could talk his way out of anything. His sister could cry if necessary. No one was going to arrest them.

"It's fine," Ian said, forcing himself to sound calm. "We'll just head back downstairs and sneak out." He grabbed Natalie's hand and they ran down the hallway. Ian flung open the door and hurled into the staircase, pulling his sister with him as he took the stairs two at a time.

"*Pas op stop!*" a deep voice echoed from a loudspeaker.

"Oh no," Natalie gasped. Her feet stopped moving and she slid down the last few steps before crashing into Ian on the landing. "It's the police."

This was not good. A security guard, they could fight off easily. But a trained police force was a different story. Ian spun on his heel and started heading back up. "We need to get to the roof."

They raced up the stairs, rounding the corner past the landing for the sixth floor. Sixteen more to go. With their head start, they wouldn't have a problem getting there before the police. But then why were the shouts getting louder?

"They'll be . . . waiting . . . for . . . us, right?" Natalie gasped, grabbing on to the railing to haul herself up onto the landing of the eleventh floor. She paused like she was going to stop and catch her breath, but there wasn't any time. Ian yanked her forward.

"Yes, of course," Ian said, forcing the words out through his burning lungs. The muscles in the backs of his legs felt like they were about to snap. But they had to keep going. The backup team would have been monitoring the alarms and would know that Ian and Natalie were in trouble. The helicopter would be there.

As they careened past the entrance to the seventeenth floor, the echo of approaching footsteps grew stronger. The police were gaining on them. He and Natalie couldn't get arrested on their first mission. If there was one thing Vikram and Isabel despised most, it was failure.

By the time they reached the top floor, Ian's wobbly legs seemed to be moving on their own, and his feet felt strangely numb. Natalie's face was bright red and she was breathing in fast, shallow gasps. He had to get her out of there.

Ian grabbed on to her small, sweaty hand and burst into the sunlight, bracing himself for the roar of the helicopter.

But the roof was completely silent.

The sky was a stunning mix of pinks and yellows, but he didn't have time to think about how picturesque the medieval towers looked in the dawn light, or how the building next door sparkled under the rising sun. All he cared about was finding the helicopter.

Ian scanned the horizon, searching for the familiar shape of the Lucian chopper, but there was nothing moving in the early-morning sky.

Someone had made a terrible mistake.

Ian could hear the stomp of police boots through the open door. They were trapped.

Unless . . .

He flung his backpack on the ground, plunged his hand inside, and removed a metal grappling hook attached to a long rope.

Natalie's eyes widened. "Oh no, no, no, no." She took a step back. "Ian, you can't. You're going to get us killed."

The door opened, releasing a stream of blue uniforms and black boots.

Natalie shrieked and clung to Ian. He raised the grappling hook over his head, swung it in a few circles, and then hurled it into the air. There was a satisfying *clank* as it caught on to the balcony jutting out from the adjacent building.

Ian twisted the end of the rope around his forearm and then wrapped his other arm around Natalie. "Come on!" They ran for the ledge. Ian felt Natalie hesitate, but she was no match for the momentum of his body weight. He leaned forward, and they tumbled over the edge.

It felt like free fall. Like they weren't attached to anything at all. Natalie screamed but Ian felt his chest cave in, as if all the air had been sucked out of him.

This had been a foolish decision.

They were going to die.

But then the rope tightened. They gained speed, but were moving sideways instead of down.

Ian felt a brief moment of relief before they slammed into a wall. This time, he yelled as a jolt of pain shook every bone in his body. The impact sent them back into the air but then they swung forward and hit the building a second time, just to the left of a large window.

He groaned and felt his body go slack. Natalie began to slide down. *"Ian!"* she screamed. He gasped and tightened his grip, hoisting her just under her arms. He wouldn't be able to hold her for long. They needed to get inside the building.

"We have to break the window," he said, struggling to speak with the effort of holding on to his sister and the rope. "Push off with your legs."

Natalie shrieked. "Ian, I'm slipping. I'm slipping!" Her voice grew hysterical.

Sweat was pouring down his arm and he felt her slide farther down. He groaned as he strained to tighten his grip. A few more inches, and she'd plummet down twenty-two stories. "Hold on!"

He kicked off from the building at an angle so that he'd hit the window on his return. But there wasn't enough force and they bounced right back off.

His arms were burning, and he could almost feel the muscle fibers breaking down. The rope cut into his hand like a knife, and the arm holding Natalie began to shake. With a groan, he pushed off the window with all this strength. They flew into the air, picking up speed on the way back. He stuck his heel out and jammed it into the glass.

Ian felt another explosion of pain as he and Natalie

tumbled through the window, landing in a heap of glass on a linoleum floor. He moaned and rolled over onto his side. Natalie lay in a crumpled heap, her hair sprinkled with glass. A trickle of blood ran down her forehead.

He pushed his hands against the floor and forced himself to sit up. "Natalie." He put his hand on her shoulder. *"Natalie!"*

His vision grew blurry and hot tears collected in his eyes, burning a path through the sweat and grime as they wound down his cheeks. "Natalie," he said, choking on the syllables.

She moaned softly and rolled over. Her eyelids twitched and then fluttered open.

"Thank God," Ian whispered.

Natalie raised herself onto her elbows and looked around. They were in another university building—some sort of administrative department. The walls were painted an uninspiring gray and ugly orange plastic chairs were arranged in clusters.

Ian helped Natalie to her feet. Although there weren't any alarms going off in this building, they needed to get out. "Let's go," he said. "The police will be here any moment."

Natalie took a step forward and winced. He knelt down and lifted her onto his back. The police had probably already surrounded the main entrances. They had to find another way out.

As he jogged down the hall, a rancid smell made him wrinkle his nose. He turned and saw a metal rubbish chute. He lowered Natalie and pulled on the handle. It looked just wide enough for them to slide down.

"Are you joking?" Natalie asked, her eyes wide with horror.

"No," he said, angling his leg so it fit inside. "Now, come on. Mum will be worried." And probably nauseated when she saw them, but that didn't matter.

Their first mission was going to be a success, even if it almost killed them.

Ian and Natalie snuck out of the rubbish room, and into the alley, then cut through a garden that looked like it led to their designated rendezvous point. Ian took his sister's hand and they limped through the gate, turning onto a quiet, tree-lined street.

It was empty. No black car was waiting for them.

Ian pulled his phone out to call Isabel. She didn't pick up. Natalie tried calling from her phone, but that didn't work, either. She left a vague message and then hung up.

"Where is she?" Natalie asked. "She said she'd be waiting here." She scanned the empty street. "Didn't she notice all the police?"

Ian closed his eyes as a rush of thoughts flooded his overworked brain. It had to be a mistake. A misunderstanding. They must not have heard Isabel correctly when they left the car. They'd probably been too nervous to pay proper attention. "I think she's meeting us . . . somewhere else," he said, opening his eyes.

"What?" Natalie's blood-streaked brow furrowed with worry. "That's not what she said."

The conversation from last night's dinner replayed through his head, sending his heart into a faster gear. And then the answer came to him. There had been something else his mother had been interested in. He pressed his lips together as he opened a web browser on his phone and typed in *Ghent altarpiece*. The first search result on the map was Saint Bavo Cathedral, about three miles away. He closed his eyes in a futile attempt to silence the thoughts rushing through his brain. "I think I know where she is."

Ian used the GPS on his phone to navigate to the cathedral. It was still early enough that the streets were mostly empty. There were no pedestrians and hardly any cars. If some of the motorists noticed the two children trudging along the twisty roads, their clothes covered in rubbish and dried blood, none of them thought to stop.

As they got closer, a mix of confusion and concern flowed through him, churning Ian's stomach like discount caviar. Part of him hoped his mother *would* be in the cathedral so they could all just go home. But another part of him dreaded finding her there. He couldn't accept the possibility that she had set them up.

Ian led Natalie around a corner and found himself in the middle of a vast square dominated by an enormous Gothic cathedral. Ian had seen countless churches, but nothing as impressive — or intimidating — as Saint Bavo. The central tower was so high Ian had to crane his neck to see the top, but the glare of the early-morning sun blocked his view.

According to his phone, it was only 6:23 Ghent time, but the enormous front door was open a crack. With a glance at Natalie, they shuffled over to the entrance and slipped through the gap, then stepped into a dim vestibule.

The air was heavy with dust and the distinct scent of old stone. Ian and Natalie scurried under a low archway and entered the main sanctuary.

For a moment, Ian could do nothing but stare in wonder. The soaring columns seemed impossibly high, supporting an arched ceiling under which shadows gathered like a perpetual twilight. Yet sunshine streamed in through the stained glass widows, dappling the floor with puddles of soft color. Ian and Natalie moved noiselessly down the black-and-white center aisle, passing dark, narrow alcoves in which various altars and sculptures glinted softly. He wasn't sure whether he was being quiet to avoid detection, or because it felt wrong to disturb the silence. It was hard to imagine the cathedral full of worshippers, let alone tourists. The stillness itself felt ancient — as if the light and the dust and the scent of the stones had been mingling together for millennia.

But then a sound broke through the quiet like a mallet, shattering the silence. A low moan that Ian felt in his bones as much as he heard it in his ears. He and Natalie followed the noise into one of the shadowy alcoves, but then jumped back, startled. Two uniformed guards were sitting back-to-back on the floor, tied together. A silk scarf had been used to gag one of them, who looked at Ian and Natalie with frantic eyes. The other man seemed unconscious.

Ian placed his hand on Natalie's shoulder and backed away slowly. A knot had begun to harden in his stomach, collecting particles of dread from throughout his body.

They made their way back up the center aisle and had almost reached the front vestibule when Ian stopped short. "What's going—" Natalie started to say, but Ian clasped his hand over her mouth.

"Shh," he whispered, and then pointed toward one of the other alcoves.

Isabel was standing in front of an enormous painting. Or, rather, a series of paintings, each depicting something vaguely religious. But Ian couldn't focus on any of the images. His brain refused to process the mass of shapes and colors. All he could see was his mother.

She wasn't on her phone, making frantic calls to the backup team. She wasn't e-mailing the British foreign secretary, placing him on a high alert.

She was examining the paintings.

Her gaze was trained on the panel in the lower left corner. Ian took a step forward, and the images snapped into focus. The painting showed a group of bald monks wearing brightly colored robes.

She reached into her purse and produced a long silver knife.

"Mum," he said, flinching as his voice echoed through the empty sanctuary, making it sound like hundreds of boys calling for their mothers.

Isabel whirled around without lowering the knife. Her skin looked pale in the ecclesiastical gloom, yet her eyes gleamed as brightly as the silver blade.

When Isabel saw their frightened faces, she brought her arm down to her side, but her expression did not soften. "What are you doing here?" she asked in a voice Ian had never heard before.

Ian felt Natalie stiffen next to him, and he knew it was up to him to explain. "Something went wrong. The code you gave us, I mean, the code we had set off an alarm. But we got the files." He reached into his pocket and removed the flash drive, holding it in his outstretched palm.

Isabel didn't seem to notice. "Where are the police? Did they follow you here?"

"At the university. They don't know we escaped."

She exhaled audibly. "Brilliant. Well done, darlings."

Ian took another step forward. "Don't you want the files?"

Isabel smiled, and suddenly, Ian felt like a child who'd just offered his mother the damp remainder of his half-chewed biscuit. "You hold on to them for now, sweetheart. I have to take care of something here before the police arrive."

"It's rubbish, isn't it?" he said, his voice fluttering up to the ceiling. "You didn't need these at all. We were just supposed to create a diversion, weren't we?" The knot in his stomach became a black hole, sucking every feeling out of him, leaving nothing behind but anger.

"Yes, and you did splendidly. I'm so proud of you." Her cool tone only infuriated him more.

"Natalie and I were almost arrested." The heat from his face trickled down his windpipe, creating a pool of smoldering rage in his chest. "We came close to killing ourselves trying to escape."

"Stop being so dramatic, darling, you look fine to me. Now, go run outside and wait in the car. I'll just be a moment." Isabel turned back to face the panel she'd been examining before. The monks were almost life-sized, and their individual faces were so distinct it looked like they were about to speak.

Isabel raised her arm so that the blade of the knife pointed toward the face of one of the monks. Ian felt his stomach twist. He knew it was only a painting, but it still looked like his mother was about to pierce real flesh.

The image of the unconscious guard flashed in his mind, followed by the terrified face of Mr. Pringle.

"No!" he shouted, lunging forward.

Isabel stepped to the side, sending Ian stumbling. "What do you think you're doing?" she hissed. "Have you gone *mad*?"

"I think he might be the only one of your family who *hasn't* gone mad."

They all spun around to see a woman standing at the edge of the alcove. The light illuminated her from behind, so all they could see was her tall silhouette. Her voice was slow and resonant. If Ian hadn't known better, he might have thought she'd just stepped out of one of the stained glass windows.

The woman stepped forward. Ian recognized her mass of gray hair and penetrating blue eyes. It was Amy's grandmother Grace Cahill.

Ian glanced back at his mother. Her jaw was clenched and she was gripping the knife so tightly her entire hand had turned white. But then she smiled, and her face transformed. "Grace," she said with exaggerated warmth, as if she were greeting a guest at a party. "What a lovely surprise. How wonderful to see you looking so . . . alive."

At first, Ian wasn't sure what Isabel was talking about, but then Grace took a few steps closer and he noticed that she was thinner than he'd ever seen her. There were deep hollows under her eyes, and her cheekbones protruded so sharply they looked like they were about to poke out through her skin. He remembered a conversation he'd overheard between his parents a few weeks ago. Something about Grace only having a few months left to live.

Yet despite her gaunt appearance, she stood just as erect as always. "Yes, well, stopping a Lucian from defacing 'The Adoration of the Mystic Lamb' was on my bucket list, so I thought I'd take a chance and pop over to Belgium." She smiled and, for a moment, the old Grace flickered into focus. "And look, here you are. Such a fortunate coincidence."

Isabel took a step toward Grace, letting the hand with the knife swing back and forth. "I knew I should have waited until after you died. The doctors gave you, what, another few weeks?"

Grace shrugged. "I've never really been one for schedules."

"Well, I was raised to believe in the importance of punctuality. And unless you turn around right now, I'm going to make sure your final departure is well on time."

Ian waited for his mother to smile, to show that she was joking, but her face remained the same. She couldn't possibly be serious. It was one thing to have someone fired or — his stomach clenched as he thought about Mr. Pringle — use other "persuasive techniques," but surely his mother wouldn't threaten to kill someone.

"I'm not so concerned about that," Grace said airily. "But I wouldn't advise you to get any closer to that painting. I have four snipers just waiting for my order to shoot."

"You're bluffing," Isabel said. Ian could tell she was trying to sound confident, but there was still an unfamiliar waver in her voice.

"I may be a lot of things, Isabel, but you know I'm not a liar."

Isabel smirked. "For all I know, those cancer drugs have addled your brain. From what I've heard, you're practically delusional."

Grace's face hardened. "That won't keep me from telling people what you really are."

Isabel took a step forward, but when her stiletto hit the tile, the *click* it made was too loud. They all jumped. It sounded exactly like a gun being cocked.

"Are you sure you want to do this?" Grace asked. "It seems like an awfully big risk to take, especially with Ian and Natalie here."

Isabel stared at her for what felt like an eternity before she finally spoke. "You're wasting your time, Grace," she said, slipping the knife back in her purse. "I can always come back. I know you're well connected, but even you won't be able to do anything from six feet underground."

"Oh, I think you'll find it very hard to get rid of me completely, Isabel."

Isabel turned to her children. "Come along, darlings." She placed a hand on Ian's shoulder and beckoned for Natalie to follow. "It's impossible to enjoy art with awful American tourists everywhere." She shot a final look at Grace. "They have no sense of decorum."

As they followed Isabel out of the alcove, Ian glanced

over his shoulder. Grace raised her eyebrows and then gave him a small nod. An odd mixture of pride and shame swept through him. He wasn't sure whether stopping his mother from stabbing the painting had been brave or incredibly foolish.

Ian blinked as he stepped into the sunlight. It was like waking up from a dream, as if the strange events inside the cathedral had occurred long ago, or perhaps not at all. He shook his head, as if to separate his real memories from the illusions. There had to be something he was missing, something that would explain what had happened.

They climbed into the car. Natalie drew her knees up to her chest and closed her eyes, though Ian was pretty sure she wasn't going to sleep. Isabel had taken out her phone and seemed to be talking to their father. "Did I wake you?" she asked. "Oh, good . . . yes . . . yes, exactly. They did brilliantly." She reached over and squeezed Ian's hand, then wiped her palm on her skirt. "Although they're in desperate need of a shower."

Ian sank back into the leather seat. His mother was proud of them. They'd done something right — even if they hadn't known the whole plan. Sitting in the warm car, the thought of cutting a piece of art seemed laughably harmless. Who cared that the figures looked like real people?

He remembered the expression on his mother's face when she'd first looked at Grace. Sometimes, being a Lucian meant you had to destroy whatever was in your way.

Grace stood in front of the altarpiece, smiling at the familiar faces. She'd come to see the "Lamb" a number of times since its return to Ghent, but it'd been many years since her last visit. She was glad for the chance to say good-bye. Grace had considered bringing Amy to show her the painting that meant so much to her, but was grateful she'd decided against it. It was better that her grandchildren know nothing about Clues or the Vespers yet.

Grace reached into her pocket and pulled out a portable X-ray device she'd built based on a prototype she "borrowed" from the Ekaterina stronghold in Cairo. She held it up to the panel Isabel had been examining and pressed a button. An image appeared on the screen. It looked almost identical to the painting, except for one key difference. There were words embroidered onto one of the saints' sleeves. A Dutch phrase. It must have been painted over at some point, because it was no longer visible to the naked eye.

Grace smiled grimly as she scanned the other panels. Each revealed another phrase. Some were in Dutch. Others were in Latin, and a few were written in languages Grace didn't recognize.

She scanned the center panel, "The Adoration of the Mystic Lamb," and inhaled sharply.

Zij zullen de aarde verplaatsen.

They will move the Earth.

So it was true.

A wave of nausea passed over her, and she stumbled, grabbing on to a wooden rail for balance. Everything she'd done, all the sacrifices she'd made to find the Clues—what was the point if the Vespers had the power to destroy them all?

Grace took a deep breath. It was time to go. She had a long trip back to Massachusetts, and she didn't want to risk missing her weekend with Amy and Dan. There weren't going to be many more of those. Although similar thoughts had passed through her mind countless times over the last few months, she still felt an ache in her chest.

She turned for one final look at the paintings her mother had loved.

Her mother had never really left her.

And Grace had no intention of leaving Amy and Dan.

"They are not only works of art. Today they are the symbols of the human spirit." President Roosevelt's words ran through Grace like someone had turned on a wireless radio inside her head.

She looked at the altarpiece and smiled. Some things were more powerful than death.

The human spirit lived on.

*Everything Grace had done,
all the sacrifices she'd
made to find the
Clues—what was the point
if the Vespers had the
power to destroy them all?*

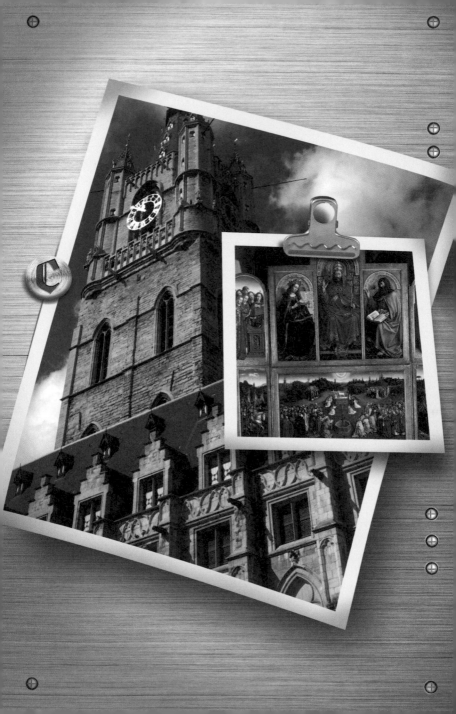